TEXAS REVENGE

TEXAS REVENGE

LAURAN PAINE

(S) SAGEBRUSH
Large Print Westerns

First published in Great Britain by Foulsham
First published in the United States by ISIS Publishing Ltd.

Published in Large Print 2005 by ISIS Publishing Ltd.,
7 Centremead, Osney Mead, Oxford OX2 0ES
United Kingdom
by arrangement with
Golden West Literary Agency

British Library Cataloguing in Publication Data
Paine, Lauran
    Texas revenge. – Large print ed. –
    (Sagebrush western series)
    1. Western stories
    2. Large type books
    I. Title
    813.5'4 [F]

ISBN 0–7531–7298–4 (hb)

Printed and bound in Great Britain by
T. J. International Ltd., Padstow, Cornwall

CHAPTER
ONE

In the Springtime,
a Richness . . .

If it hadn't been for the way a gentle breeze blew against her, Forge probably wouldn't have noticed CarrieLee Dolan at all. She was slender, but what he saw in that long look was the moulding of her body. The firm, subtle roundness of it. Not flat and lean with abrupt angles like a man's body, at all. He stood there with his horse's reins in his hands, just looking.

There was an angry set to CarrieLee's jaw where she stood beside the creek staring back at him, an unfriendly light in her eyes. She had seen him before but his height hadn't been noticeable then, because she'd never seen him off a horse before. Now it was, and furthermore his shoulders were too wide for the size of his hips. There were bunches under his shirt, too. They might be muscle but they were lumpy and ugly looking just the same. But mostly, she resented his manner; his long, unblinking stare. Its candour indicated crudeness. She stood erect and stared right back.

1

Forge knew who she was, but he hadn't ever considered her more than a kid before. It was startling what a year or two could do to a girl. He was astonished to find her so pretty and feminine, up close. In spite of her expression now, and the storminess of her eyes, she was very handsome.

Her eyes were large, with a world of expression in them, only now they were shadowed under the lowering clouds of her eyebrows, made darker looking. Her mouth, too, wasn't the same. It was fuller, with a lilting curve to it. It made him think of music, for some abstract reason he didn't bother to puzzle out. Even with the disapproval and antagonism in her face, she was very, very, pretty.

He wanted to say something. It wasn't every early spring day that he jumped off his horse here to drink at the creek and saw a vision like CarrieLee Dolan standing there.

But the words wouldn't come. He even lowered his gaze and tried to think of something, but the moment had lasted too long. There was a great wall of awkwardness between them now. He gave it up, finally, but he did nod, then he turned, swung into the saddle, wheeled his horse and rode back out into the new day.

CarrieLee stood there with her inner tumult long after he had ridden off. She knew who he was because he had hollered out to her several times and waved as he'd loped by, homeward bound from Fontaine. He'd waved with the exuberance of any young cowboy and up until this year she'd always waved back. Forge

2

Windsor, a Pothook rider. One of that wild brood Will Leeman hired.

She turned finally and went down along the creek towards her father's cabin.

Tim Dolan, trapper, buffalo hunter — grand old patriarch of a forgotten race — one of the last of the oldtime Mountain Men. But time had a way of drawing out the pride and ferocity, the wildness and the recklessness. Tim Dolan with his tiny blue eyes like ice chips and his reduced living — his muskrat trapping and his private world of dim, grey memories — was CarrieLee's father.

And anyway, she'd teach that Forge Windsor to stare. She'd never speak to him again. And — he'd talk about her. All cowboys talked about women. Well, she'd cut him off so hard the next time they met he'd be forever getting over it. Him and his staring and his talk!

She didn't forget his look in the warming days that followed with their high, hurrying clouds, either. She let it torment her deliberately, and she planned a female way of getting even with him.

Her idea devolved around the fact that the country was raw and new. Mostly, the Indians were pushed farther west now. There were only occasional riders who stopped by at dusk or spent the night in the little horse shed, and neighbours were miles apart. People were starved for one another's company, so every three or four months there was a gathering in Fontaine. Camp-meetings, they were called.

And for every camp-meeting CarrieLee could remember, she had scrubbed until her skin shone and braided her taffy hair and sat perfectly still in agonised expectancy while her father harnessed his old saddlehorse to their rickety buggy. The drive in had always been slow torture and Fontaine at camp-meeting time was purest enchantment. She had always loved those get-togethers and she knew the Pothook riders did, too.

Everyone went. There were picnics and horse racing, singing, tests of strength, shooting matches, and even dancing. There were also ladies with big hats with purple feathers in them.

So she watched the days go by like she always did when the time was getting near, but with a vindictive purposefulness that was new to her. She had a plan. She'd show that gawking cowboy something! She did, too.

Forge noticed her again at the camp-meeting. Remembering her as a pig-tailed kid in years past, he saw now a beautiful girl in her developed estate. Alluring and frightening at the same time.

She seemed not to notice him. It hurt him deep within where he could feel the pain but couldn't control it. He didn't stare this time though. Rather he eyed her surreptitiously, craftily, with a delicious slyness.

Then he went out to race a Pothook horse Will Leeman had brought in from the ranch, and he won. But what affected him more than the winning was that she was standing by his side, speaking, when he was still breathing fast, eyes aglow, turned away from the shouts and howls of the crowd.

"Did you stare your way through the race, too?" she said.

Colouring darkly, he looked into her eyes. Up close, they were large, liquid-looking, and grey. The steady look scared him worse than any Indian ever had. Made his insides draw up as though from a blow. He almost stammered.

"I didn't mean to stare that day, ma'm."

He was contrite because he didn't know what else to be, but he didn't like it.

"Well, you rode a good race," she said carelessly, with casual coolness; some instinctive female intuition telling her how to do this. Wrap him up and dump him in the churned yellow dust at her feet, figuratively.

"That's a good horse," he said slowly, looking past her a little so that a mite of her spell was broken. "We don't use him for much but racing. Anyway, he's too high-strung to work cattle off of."

"Did you tell your friends about staring at me over by the creek?"

"Shucks," he said, looking down into her grey eyes again, "that's nothing to talk about, Miss." Then his eyes twinkled at her in their bluest depths. "You sure looked pretty that day."

She blushed and he thought she was the most lovely thing he had ever seen, her derelict old father and the sagging old cabin notwithstanding. She moved away with triumph like a clear-toned bell, ringing in her mind.

Afterwards, she was a little aloof, but never cold, and her trap was set perfectly. She knew it in the days that followed when he rode over to the cabin every now and then to visit. He'd sit respectfully and listen to old Tim, and her father loved having him as an audience.

She would smile guilelessly at him and be almost convulsed with laughter that she hid behind a serene, disinterested expression, when Tim would launch into some particularly long-winded story, and she would tiptoe discreetly out of the house leaving them together. Then Forge's face would grow long and troubled. She had brought him to heel all right.

He began to come regularly and by then her malice was gone. She would watch him ride up with his boyish grin and swing down and approach her with his direct gaze, and from that she knew she had her victory — but then what? She had come to like him and knew he liked her, too, but of a sudden she no longer had the initiative.

Aggressively, in some way she didn't fathom, he had taken the lead. It was obvious in the ways he found to be alone with her. Brief moments when little was said, that she re-lived vividly in her mind, afterwards. The look in his frank eyes, the softness of his laugh and the closeness of his masculine strength.

And she was waiting for his love a long time before he told her of it, haltingly, almost shame-facedly, and that happened one Sunday when they went up along the crushed-grass trail by the creek. In May, it was. May, 1856. They were walking through the sparkling, early afternoon, later, when he said, "Wait, CarrieLee. Don't walk so fast."

She had slowed. "All right." Then she had almost held her breath with a sensation of weakness and alarm overcoming her.

They had seen enough of each other by then so that their awkwardness was gone. Neither was troubled much by old Tim Dolan's speculative glances any more, either. They shared a ripening understanding that went well beyond the wonderings of Tim and the Pothook riders, who weren't blind either.

He wanted to talk about those things but they were hard to put into words. You felt them but couldn't say them because it just never came out right.

Instead, he reached for her there in the shade and privacy of the graceful, leafy willows with their intoxicating scent of richness. Took her in his arms and felt almost reverent towards the velvety firmness of her — the warmth — and kissed her. She was against him, unmoving, eyes closed.

He asked, simply, "Why do you close your eyes, CarrieLee?"

"Oh — ," she said. "I don't know." There was a pause; then, "Because I don't want you to see what's in them, Forge."

He raised one hand and tilted her head back with it but she closed her eyes and only a soft shadow lurked below the dark sweep of her lashes. He felt closed out of her world and it baffled him a little, so, boyishly, he said, "Why don't you look up here, CarrieLee? Open your eyes and look at me."

She kissed him and moved her face a little. Ran it along his cheek and pushed her nose in against the soft place just above his collarbone, and answered him.

"I love you too much, Forge, that's why. It'll show."

"Well," he said, "I love you, too." As though that made everything all right.

"It's different. If I kept my eyes open it'd make me feel — naked."

That shocked him but he laughed at her with a little bit of understanding, too, then he grew solemn and looked out of the willows and across the creek. Out over the endless prairie where large, dark shadows moved across the cresting, new grass, chained to the high clouds they followed forever. Cloud-shadows.

"I've loved you a long time, CarrieLee, but saying it is the hardest thing I ever did."

She nodded her head with a swift movement of understanding and said nothing. Didn't even move although the backs of her legs were hurting from standing up like that, bending inward a little.

"You too?"

"Yes."

"Then you shouldn't care if it shows."

"I don't now, Forge. If you feel the same way, then I don't care."

He groped for her elbows and held her out from him. She could see the thin white line above his upper lip and the turbulence in his clear blue eyes. His hands went higher, to her shoulders. They shook a little but the trembling died out when he gripped her.

There was a little pain to his biting, strong hold on her shoulders but she savoured it and twisted slightly to make it more intense, because this was real.

This hurting was reality and everything else, the talk, the fragrance, the sunshine and shadows, were confusion. But this pain coming out of him was reality.

And they didn't stop after that. The exquisite hurting was enough; more, really, than either had hoped for. They were swept away with their discovery and lost in it.

Later, she watched the lowering sun in the west splash a reddish tint over his brown hair, and reached up with her hands to brush it away from his forehead. This was the moment of choked-up, hushed lassitude. Peace.

"I'll stake a claim," he said quickly, but with a wryness in his voice, like there was in his eyes.

Squatters. Every rider, every cowman, scorned squatters. They lived no better than Indians. There was no other way now, though. He stared into the ground with a fierce intensity. He'd squat and they'd fight their way up from that and be cattle people. In his youthfulness he saw life like that. Sweat made everything right. Hard, grunting labour, and sweat. He was young.

"We'll stake a claim along the creek. I'll build you a cabin. We'll get some cattle." Then, with quick savageness and total irrelevance, he said, "CarrieLee, it hurts. I love you so much it hurts. Honest — right here." He touched his body vaguely because he wasn't sure just where the ache was, but it was there all right.

She pulled his head down to her with both hands and kissed him. There was a shiny gloss to her eyes; a deep, lazy restedness.

"Forge? We don't have to stay here, do we?" Then she laughed when he looked startled. "No; I don't mean right here — right now. I meant out here on the prairie, so far from everywhere, with nothing but grass and distance and loneliness."

His glance didn't move from her face. There was a strange vacantness, an inwardness, to it. Here? In the grass and distance? He had never questioned the future. He had thought of it in a vague way. He had plans of his own for a herd, some day. Land, horses, a ranch — but they were obscure things in his mind. But there had never been any doubts either, about staying on the land. It was a good place, here; washed with sunlight and soft with grass and space. Things of the spirit; of the soul and heart. He was strong, too. Someday . . .

He tried to explain it to her but, like love, it was hard to find the right words. His brother had a claim up in the sagebrush hills. He told her about that because it seemed the most suitable way for a Windsor to live, and also because his brother had a wife and now he'd have one, too. The sense of kinship was drawing him closer to his ideal, and he completely forgot what he'd ridden over to tell her, in the first place, as he talked, now. Rambled, feeling for words that barely touched the fringe of the way he really felt.

"Forge; I know claims," she said finally. "I want something better than a claim and a log house for you and me."

He was silenced and deeply troubled. A melancholy breeze blew over the embers of his passion. "Is there anything better? We can have it as good as we'll work to make it."

"In Fontaine the houses have wooden floors," she said. "There are people there, too."

"Fontaine?" he said. "What would I do there? CarrieLee, I'm a rider." The pride of every horseman from the beginning of time was in his words. The scorn of the mounted for those who trudged afoot. "I don't know a town trade. We'd be unhappy in a town, I know we would."

She tried to explain it to him while he lay against her with her arms around him. He could learn a trade; work for a shopkeeper maybe. He was strong — perhaps a blacksmith would take him on. She wanted to leave the prairie, the drudgery of hauling water and the hollowness of forever being lonely. They came very close to quarrelling over it.

"Maybe you'd of been better off with a town man," he said. "I don't understand you, CarrieLee. You've always been out here. We're free; we're our own bosses." He was straining against her arms, in his ire.

She watched the storm gathering and pulled herself up close to him. He relaxed and she held him gently. The sky was getting redder up through the filigree of willow leaves. She stared up at it. His stubborn anger had frightened her.

"Forge — I want you — that's all; just you. But I thought we'd be happier, maybe . . ." It trailed off and he made no answer at all. She couldn't see the latent winteriness in his eyes nor the blunt set of his jaw.

Forge Windsor would never soften. CarrieLee Dolan would find that out.

She held him and crooned to him, rocking him a little. It worked. The anger was coaxed out of him. Then, satisfied, she moved reluctantly.

"We'd better go back. It's time for dad's supper. He'll be wondering."

They went back but Tim was busy oiling traps and hardly more than glanced at them as they went past him into the house. Forge felt stifled inside. He walked back out into the early dusk and dropped down beside the old man.

"Tim; a man can do worse than stay in this country, can't he?"

It was more a statement than a question. Tim Dolan swung his weathered face with its old lines and seams, like the erosion gullies in the distant mountains. His grey eyes, sunken and brooding beneath shaggy, monolithic eyebrows, regarded the cowboy in a pensive way, then he nodded his head and watched the grass bow before the rolling whisper of an evening breeze, far out.

"I reckon he can," Tim said. " 'Course — it's a man's land, Forge. Women — 'ceptin' Injun women of course — got little liking for it." His long ensuing silence was more eloquent of deep meaning than his words could ever be.

"I married me a woman new t'the land. She loved it. There aren't many like that, especially now." He fell silent again and Forge was too far down in his well of inner turmoil to keep the conversation going.

12

He rode back to Pothook not long after that. They had eaten — bear meat, wild onions, barley pudding — and there had been a stillness at the table that was thick enough to lean against. CarrieLee had walked out with him and stood aside as he saddled up. She watched his movements like she always had, but said nothing until he turned and bent swiftly to kiss her.

"Forge? Are you sorry?"

"Sorry? No, why should I be sorry? I love you an awful lot, that's all. I've got that in my head. That and the things we talked about. They've got to be thought out."

"When will you be back?"

He drew the reins through his fingers, looking at them. "As soon as I can. Will's making up a crew to go over into Texas and fetch back a herd of she-stock." He raised his eyes. "That's what I came over to tell you today — and never did."

Her heart knew a sudden heaviness. "How long will it take, Forge?" The words were very calm, almost gentle, the way she said them. It matched the level gaze of her eyes.

"I don't rightly know, CarrieLee," he answered. "I've never made the trek before. Some of the boys say maybe two months; I don't know."

"Well — kiss me good-bye, anyway."

He did. He kissed her softly with the dull pain rising anew inside him, then he swung up and looked down at her with a solemn and indefinable strangeness, wheeled the Pothook horse and rode off.

She stood there looking after him until the last muted, grass-deadened echo was lost in the lowering night. The heaviness was greater. She had an urge to go two places at the same time. An almost overpowering restlessness plagued her. Go back to the little willow-lined glade where they had been, by the creek, or just start out walking across the flatness towards the far-away hills where a sea of sagebrush made them forever purple, with silver edgings when the sun was just right. Walk until she was lost — absorbed into the bigness of the Universe.

She did neither. After a while she went back to the cabin and listlessly cleaned up after supper. Her father's pipe made a tangy, wild smell in the house. It drew her back to normalcy and reality for it was an old, familiar smell; a homely odour.

She wished she dared tell old Tim. Dared to sit down by him before the mud fireplace and talk it out where he could hear and listen. But that was clearly impossible, so she kept her own council and nursed the sweetest of all her pleasurable memories in her heart.

In the springtime there was a richness in the land, in the air and the grass. In the sky-clouds, and now in her as well. A treasure never to be experienced like that again. An overwhelming richness of her spirit and soul, her heart and mind and body.

Forge didn't come back. She knew he was gone to Texas with the wild Pothook men. It added to her deepening loneliness; was reflected in her quietness and the gravity, the deepening shadows under her eyes.

14

Then, three weeks later, Tim Dolan lifted his shaggy head over breakfast and fixed her with a shrewd eye.

"Honey, I got to go down to Abilene. You care to go?"

The surprise of his offer — she had never, in sixteen years, known him to leave the Fontaine country — caught her unawares. A little breathlessly, she said, "I'd love to, Dad. When?"

"Oh — tomorrow."

He tossed it off casually and that shook her too, so, the following morning when she felt sick after arising, she knew it was the excitement. Gratefully, she felt the lightening of her light-headedness, and plunged into the work of getting ready for the trip.

They locked up the cabin, hitched up old Ute, put two bundles of clothing in the back of the buggy and started off. Their sleeping robes were lashed against some pans for cooking and thus there was only the dry, crunching sound of the wheels to break the silence that engulfed them.

Tim chewed tobacco and sat hunched forward with a sombre thoughtfulness on his wrinkled face. CarrieLee lived every second. Her excitement wouldn't abate. It grew considerably, in fact, after they left Fontaine behind, because that was the only town she had ever known.

The next morning she was giddy again. Weak and unsettled in the stomach and light-headed again. That time Tim noticed it and showed concern.

"Cuss it; I never should've done it. It's too far a drive for ye, CarrieLee."

15

She smiled and waited for the spell to pass. "I'll be all right, Dad. Fetch some water for the pans, will you?"

That was the last time she felt dizzy. They went drifting down the flatness, like leaves blown in autumn. The cloud-shadows scurried before them. The spring-time was bursting with life and wherever they came close to creeks there were leafy willows and cottonwoods. A musty, heavy fragrance filled the air. Life was good. There was promise. God was everywhere except in Abilene.

Her first glimpse of the bustle, the frantic activity and the noise, was disappointing. Then came the smells and the riotous clashing of colours that was Abilene. She was both frightened and excited.

Old Tim gazed tolerantly on the place. His throat was warm and dry and his thirst was stirring. Ghosts of decades gone were beckoning to him. Calling silently with their heads thrown back and their eyes afire. "Abilene," he said suddenly. "I knew it when it wasn't nothin'."

She almost said it isn't much now, but she didn't. Certainly Fontaine was cleaner, quieter. Still, this was a town known all over the country. It had a wicked name then, but in twenty, thirty years, it would be far worse.

Then she was in it, absorbed by the clamour, the colour and the bedlam. And the people. They were everywhere and not all were cowmen either. There were startlingly handsome men, and women in brocaded clothing, unbelievable hats, dresses that were appallingly expensive looking. She had to catch her breath when Tim drew up under a shade tree and tied Ute, leaned back on the buggy seat and gazed over at her with a crooked, sad little smile.

"Here we be, honey," he said. "There here's civilisation." He watched the ebb and flow of humanity with no great interest. "You walk around a bit and see the sights. I'll meet ye back here at the buggy in an hour or two. 'That what ye want?"

"Yes," she said, her first disappointment past and her interest stirring sharply. "It's — different — isn't it?"

He didn't answer. Just laughed his easy, tolerant laugh and got down rather stiffly, watching her stand with uncertainty beside the buggy, eyes large and sparkling. He'd never seen her look so vital, so alive and mature and — well — just plain pretty as a picture, before. Then she began to move off.

In mid-town there was a big wooden store building where people flowed both ways at the doorway. Within, was a smell of oiled flooring and spices. There were bolts of gay cloth and things she could only guess a reason for their existing at all. Farther on were saloons and loitering men. There was a rare sprinkling of blanket-Indians, too, and men with fringed shirts of elk-skin and buck-skin, but these she ignored. Fontaine had them. The women who swept by her had a heavenly scent that didn't come from lye-soap.

Passing a better class saloon, she swung wide to avoid two men who came swinging out. One went around her, in front, while the other man swung past, behind her. Both were heading towards the long hitchrail with the cribbing-marks deep in its stout tie-log and she turned to watch one of them.

He had the whitest hat she had ever seen on a man or a woman. Snow white. It was soft looking, too, not like the hats she saw the riders wear back home. It was low-crowned and flat-brimmed like a rider's hat, but it was softer and startlingly white.

He was a tallish man with jet black hair and eyes to match. His trousers were tight and showed handsome legs. His boots were dust-coated but soft too, not like the stiff, cowhide boots other men wore along the frontier. Then, there were two heavily silvered guns around his lean waist, and that surprised her. Silver inlay in intricate designs; the guns were fabulous. One had a Mexican eagle — a fierce-looking bird with a writhing snake in its mouth — emblazoned on the handle of the weapon.

The details of the man with the white hat so engrossed her that she forgot the man himself, and flushed in mortification when he turned, faced her, and bent just a little from the waist. Then she looked up with terrible embarrassment and saw his face. It was handsome and the eyes glowed darkly. There was a thin, high-bridged nose and a ruddy look in the cheeks on each side of the long, thin, mouth. "Ma'm," he said in a strong sounding voice, "you must recognise me, but I'm sorry to say I don't recollect you at all."

The other man, leaner, taller, fairer, with one gun and a hardness to his eyes to match the wariness of his expression, looked up from where he was untying his horse. He spoke dryly. "The kid's just staring, Mark. Leave her be."

The two-gun man's face dissolved into a smile. "A country kid, huh? By God but you're a pretty one, though," he said.

CarrieLee felt his hand on her arm. She tried to swing away but the hand drew her back around. Terror was in her, and chagrin. He couldn't be ignored so she faced him, tugging gently at her sleeve. He didn't release her.

"Let go of my arm," she said very coldly, with a wood-smoke shade to her glance.

"Not yet," he said.

Then she swung with her free hand. The impulse had been swift and demanding; she had obeyed it. Her palm struck him sharply, stingingly, across the cheek.

The taller man at the hitchrail leaned on the gnawed stringer with both hands and bent over with laughter. "Good for you, kid," he said. "Good for you. He asked for it."

The two-gun man's beautiful white hat had fallen into the dust. His black eyes shone like well-water at midnight. He put one hand to his face, the other still clung to her arm. CarrieLee swung away to flee. His grip checked her up short. She tried to yank away, tore at the strong fingers with her free hand.

"Let go!" she gasped, twisting savagely. "You let me go!"

The man at the hitchrail was watching. His amused look died slowly. There was an opaque stillness in his glance. He said, "Let her go, Mark. She's just a country kid. You've scared her to death."

"I'm *not* a kid — I'm a woman!"

"Dogged if you aren't," the two-gun man said, dropping his hand from his face. He hadn't expected such an explosive climax to a casual meeting. Still holding her arm he made another little bow from the waist with the same mocking smile. "Where do you live?"

"A long way from here. *Will* you let me go?"

"Yes," he said, "but where are you staying in Abilene?"

"Why?" she demanded, relaxing against his grip and giving him stare for stare.

"So we can walk you home, ma'm," the two-gun man said very quietly, his eyes steady on her face. "I'm Mark Belleau. That's Stan Stryker. Where, ma'm?"

"I can go back by myself, thank you."

"No," Belleau said with a negative and solemn shake of his head. "This is Abilene. You were just lucky to get this far." He turned towards the tall man leaning over the hitchrail. "Isn't that right, Stan?"

Stryker seemed on the verge of a smile, but instead he nodded his head at her. "Well," he said dryly. "Abilene's not the best town for girls to be walking around loose in, ma'm."

"There," Belleau said triumphantly, releasing her arm. "Come on. We'll all go together."

CarrieLee looked over at the taller, fairer man. He was amused again. She felt an instinctive liking for him. He was strong but not flamboyant. There was something still and calm in his half-grinning look. He had eyes as clear and blue as Forge's eyes. He was

20

waiting with deliberate patience and a twinkle in his eyes, for her next move.

"But I was just walking," she said finally. "Just seeing — things."

Neither man showed any surprise. Belleau even nodded his head as though she had given the correct answer to his unspoken thoughts.

"Then I reckon we'll just do it together. Come on, Stan — other thing can wait."

She watched the larger man come across the scuffed plankwalk and fall in on her right while the two-gun man retrieved his soiled white hat, clapped it on his head without a glance, and led off.

Belleau was talkative. He gestured freely with one hand. He gave way before none of the other foot traffic and stared down those who appeared to resent their threesome, which forced a lot of people off into the thick dust of the roadway as the two men escorted CarrieLee over Abilene.

"That's the Federal Eagle, a saloon and a hotel. Over there're the trading corrals. You can sometimes trade for a horse over there and when you go to look at him, by God he'll be the same one someone stole from you the night before." Both Stryker and Belleau laughed at that. CarrieLee smiled.

"Over there's the wagon works. Only one on the frontier, I'm told. And here, beside Stan there, that's the cafe where Pard Dugan got killed last year. Shot in the back o' the head while he was eating."

"Who was he?" CarrieLee asked innocently.

21

Belleau's dark eyes grew round. "You never heard of Pard Dugan? Why, he was the best horsethief in the west, Miss — Miss — say; you never told us your name."

She smiled at him. "You never asked it."

Stan Stryker chuckled. He wasn't as gay as Belleau, but there was a restrained pleasantness about him. He said, "She's learning, Mark. By suppertime she'll have you tied up and tossed."

Belleau threw back his head and laughed. His teeth were very white and handsome. "All right — I'm asking you now. What is it?"

"CarrieLee Dolan. We live at a place called Fontaine. It's — out a ways."

"CarrieLee," Mark said, then repeated it. "That's a very pretty name. It fits a very pretty girl." He must have seen the way her smile dimmed because he swung away and resumed his other role again with an out-thrown arm and an exaggerated wave.

"And that — over there. That's the Crystal House. It's a theatre."

"A theatre? Where they have actors?" She was shocked. All of the iniquity of life was centred where players acted. She'd been taught that up until she was eight years old, when her mother had died. The dim, forbidding memories stayed. Stan was looking down at her with silent amusement. Mark looked at her with less amusement than wonder. His glance, keen and sharp, saw the dismay. He stopped in mid-stride, let his arms drop as though suddenly faced with something incomprehensible, and frowned a little, so that a vertical, deep furrow appeared between his black eyes, then he made a resigned, loud sigh.

"Haven't you ever seen actors before? Don't they have them in Fontaine?"

"Of course not. I've never seen a theatre before. Anyway . . ."

"Then you will see them play tonight."

"Don't be ridiculous." Her glance was withering. It rolled off him like water.

"Ridiculous?" He shot an appealing glance at Stryker. "What's ridiculous about players and acting?"

"It's — well — ." She knew they'd both laugh at her so she didn't finish it.

"It's still too early though, so we'll walk a little more, then we'll eat — then we'll go to the playhouse."

He left her no chance to deny such a suggestion, but took her arm lightly and strolled on again, speaking with the swift, easy way he had. Stan Stryker trouped along in his pleasant-faced silence.

When they had seen all of Abilene, Mark steered them to a hotel where the food was almost as good as it was said to be, and they ate amid the jostle, the strange, gamey smells of the place — and the people — with CarrieLee's eyes as large as spur rowels.

A huge old fireplace of sandstone, black and cavernous looking, was tended by a little negro who turned an iron spit with buffalo roasts skewered to it. His dark face glistened from the twofold heat and his white teeth and rolling eyes made an amusing contrast to the ebony sheen of him.

CarrieLee was enthralled. She had to revise her first impression of Abilene. There was high colour in her cheeks and breathless enchantment in her grey eyes, larger than ever, and luminous. When they were finished, Mark's dark gaze was unmoving in his regard of her.

"Now," he said, "we still have something to show you. The view of Abilene from the air."

"The air?" CarrieLee echoed, wondering, feeling a stirring of uneasiness and excitement.

Mark didn't let her wonder long. He got up, flung silver on the table and smiled. "Come on." He was purposefully avoiding Stryker's glance, which had gone somewhat hard and flat.

He led the way to the narrow, gloomy staircase sandwiched between two buildings, and led her up to the second floor of the place, where the light was no better, threw open a door and ushered her straight across the room to a window that was open. There he beamed again.

"Now — see what it looks like from up here."

CarrieLee had never been above earth level before. The panorama was indeed thrilling. She was totally unconscious of the duel of eyes that went on behind her back. Warm, flashing black eyes and chilled, disapproving, blue ones.

"It's — so — different, from up here. It's — I never saw a town from the air before."

She was turning away from the window when she saw something familiar. It made her heart sink with a sick feeling. Her father, back at the buggy, sprawled in the seat, mouth open, face flushed, sound asleep — drunk.

Tim Dolan drunk. It wasn't a new sight but it was always an illusion-shattering one. She turned away with her hurt rebelliousness showing. Mark was watching her closely and Stan was standing back a ways with his head down and his thumbs hooked in his cartridge belt.

"I — thank you very much — both of you — but I've got to get back now."

It caught the two-gun man off balance. He had expected any mood but this sudden change to morbidness. Anger again, possibly another slap in the face, anything — but not this. He was, for once, at a loss.

Stan studied her from his unmoving eyes. He sensed it was something she had seen. With a long stride he crossed to the window and gazed up the way she had been looking. The old gaffer in the countryman's buggy with the greying old Indian horse. Sure; that would be it. He turned back with a little of his own resentment showing. Old fool; bring a girl like this one to a hell-hole like Abilene — then pass out and leave her alone. Ought to be horsewhipped.

Mark broke the gloom. "Well — there's still the last surprise." He turned and went back out of the room, down the stairs and out into the gathering dusk. His black eyes sought out the little carriage lantern that glimmered weakly. The theatre was open for business. He swung back and took CarrieLee's arm and smiled quickly at her.

"You'll never forget this, either."

He piloted her through the roadway traffic, up onto the boardwalk and down to the very front of the Crystal House. She resisted his tug there, and scowled very positively into his face. Before she could speak though, three things happened. One, she could see old Tim from there. The pain and resentment dug deeper into her heart. Then a man went into the theatre with a pretty woman on his arm. And, finally, Stan Stryker's face — a little like Forge's, especially up around the eyes — smiled down at her.

"It's all right," he said. "We'll all three be together."

The players wore tights. That was the first thing that made her feel like hiding. The second thing was that they kissed up there on the stage in plain sight of everyone. That happened in the scene of their play-acted marriage after they had foiled the gun-bearing villain. But she wanted to drop right through the floor when the lady came back with a doll in her arms to represent the fruit of their play-marriage.

But, if the play horrified her, the theatre itself didn't. There weren't many lights except up by the stage, but there were a lot of people. Women as well as men, and no one seemed particularly drunk or lewd or boisterous. She felt a naughty sense of satisfaction, too, when she was aware of other people looking at both her escorts. It was warming to her mind to be noticed by these people in their city clothes. There was a feeling of well-being in that.

Once, Mark reached over, took her hand and squeezed it, then let it go and she folded her hands together, interlocking the fingers. But even that had been a thrill, although she didn't want it repeated.

CHAPTER
TWO

In the Summer, the Changing of a Spirit...

Old Tim had forgotten CarrieLee. He had dismissed her from his mind when he went through the saloon's doorway where the musty and masculine, rank and welcome fumes closed down over him. It had been a terribly long time . . .

The amount of whisky he swallowed didn't heighten his sense of responsibility naturally. For a little while out of the years he wanted to be a part of the noise and personality of a genuine Abilene saloon, and he was.

But he didn't get so drunk he couldn't find old Ute and the buggy. Nor did he forget to buy the old horse a thick flake of prairie hay and a bait of barley. But after that all he wanted was to crawl up on the seat and be left strictly alone. He was; Abilene didn't care.

He slept away the day and awakened with the darkness and, still unmindful of his daughter, he got down off the seat and shambled back towards the saloon again.

There were a lot of stores to pass by first, though, so he gawked as he walked. There was even a theatre with people emptying from it. Women even, and men in tall hats with curly beards. Lots of people — good God! CarrieLee!

He stopped like a horse hauled up short. He stared uncertainly, unbelievingly. A man couldn't always trust his eyes when he was in a big town.

"Dad."

"CarrieLee!" It *was* her, coming out of that playhouse. Wrath came with the passing shock. Indignation. "What were you doin' in *there*!" The doubts came and turned to reality in his foggy mind. "CarrieLee! You get to the . . ."

He never got to finish it. A man's hand closed down over his shirt and propelled him up the plankwalk through the crowds. The face above had frosty blue eyes.

"Your daughter's all right," the tall young man said crisply. "Now watch your language. Don't spoil what fun she's had this afternoon any more'n you already have."

Mark and CarrieLee caught up and Mark, with a dark, lingering look at Tim, said, "Come on; let's get out of the crowd." He too was mindful of CarrieLee's embarrassment.

"I'll not move," Tim said, bolstering himself by a wall. His sunken grey eyes were baleful when they swung fully on his daughter. "You! I should've known!"

The blue-eyed stranger growled at him again with menace in his glance but it was the two-gun man who spoke. "He needs something to eat. Come along."

He started to turn away but CarrieLee caught his arm. Her eyes were deeply grateful. "No. You've already done enough. I'll take him to the buggy."

Mark looked from CarrieLee to her adamant father. He had an ugly little shine to his sidelong glance at Dolan, then he straightened fully around.

"Nope. We'll get him fed, then you can have him."

They went back to the same place to eat and CarrieLee never had a more miserable supper in her life. It was purest agony. Old Tim berated the younger men incessantly until she could hardly stand to sit there any longer. She got up swiftly and hurried towards the door. Mark looked surprised, raised his eyebrows at Stan, got up and went after her. The blue-eyed man gazed reprovingly at drunken Tim, and said nothing, just drew in his mouth a little.

"CarrieLee — wait!"

He caught up with her where she was turning off the plankwalk and hurrying over beside the old buggy with the drowsing horse between the shafts.

"Wait. He doesn't know what he's saying, kid. Give him a . . ."

"I'm *not* a kid." She was perilously close to tears. The darkness and her averted face hid it from him.

He felt like swearing or hitting someone. "The old fool," he said. Then he took her hand and drew her over beside the buggy and boosted her up to the seat. She felt terrible. Completely wretched. Her own father — the only person . . .

"We'll sober him up, honey. Don't let it spoil your day. Listen," he stole his arm around her waist and drew inward a little, "we'll get a room for the two of you in our hotel and put him to bed. That's what he needs; sleep."

She didn't fight the arm. It seemed like it belonged there, right then. She pulled her head around with an effort and stared at him. He was kind. She hadn't thought so at first, but he was; especially now.

Mark misinterpreted the look. "Don't be afraid," he said.

"I'm not," she said quietly. "Only — you've been so nice and it'll come to a lot of expense and all."

He laughed. It was a boyish, rich laugh, like Forge Windsor's laugh was, only a little louder. He jumped down off the seat and held up a hand for her.

"Come on. We'll have it all fixed up in nothing flat."

They did, but old Tim protested right up to the moment the two men had him safely bedded down, then he gazed up at them dubiously, the small grey eyes quizzical.

"Why're ye doin' this, lads? Ye owe me nothing."

Stan answered in a calm way. "Did you ever do something for someone you didn't *have* to do?"

Tim thought on it for a long moment, then he sighed and nodded his head. "I reckon. I'm obliged to ye," then he fell into a deep, alcoholic slumber.

Mark and Stan went back to their room. CarrieLee was waiting. They both smiled at her. A big flood of relief showed swiftly in her face. She sat down in a chair and smiled back at them and Mark went to the old chifferobe and dug out a glass of dark red wine. Very sombrely he poured three glasses, handed them

30

around, then grinned out of his midnight-black eyes at CarrieLee.

"To Tim Dolan — the man who slept here, and by so doin' left you to charm us a little longer — CarrieLee."

She had never tasted wine and didn't want to now, but after all they had done . . . It was sweet, too, and went down easily. She didn't remember where she'd gotten it, but somewhere in the back of her mind was an idea that all intoxicants were awful tasting. This wasn't; in fact, this was very pleasant. Glowingly pleasant. Warmly pleasant. Her eyes livened up. She told them about Fontaine, about the cabin by the creek and the miles of prairie that ran abruptly into the wrinkled hills where the purple sea of sage was.

And they listened until Stan put down his glass and said he'd go take their horses to the liverybarn. He stood at the door for a moment, working the latch and throwing a long, significant look back at Mark. The dark-eyed man threw back his head and laughed, then Stan looked rueful. He left without saying anything.

Mark poured her a little more of the sweet wine. It went down even smoother, then he moved over beside her chair and knelt. His dark eyes were perfectly still now, like a black night in autumn. No movement, no expression — or *all* expression — she didn't know which even after he had his arm around her again.

He kissed her. It was a stirring experience. A strangely reminiscent experience but she was passive at first because it wasn't right.

He moved closer and kissed her again and it was different that time. It stirred up a tempest within her,

31

an ardour that made her respond. She stood up and he came up with her. Her arms went up around his neck. They stood like that a long, tingling moment, then he released her gently and stood back smiling at her.

"CarrieLee — I can't just let you walk out of my life now. You can see that, can't you? I just can't."

His words bewildered her. "What else is there to do?"

His answer was to sweep her into his arms again. That time the fire in her own blood raced. She sought his mouth with her own. They were like that when Stan opened the door and stood framed there, his questioning eyes chilling gradually, his eyebrows lifting a little in a bleak way. Mark released her and smiled. Stan came in and closed the door. He leaned against it, ignoring CarrieLee. There was an appearance of waiting in his stance.

"Well?" Mark said challengingly.

"Well," Stan said quietly. "I reckon she'd better get down to her own room."

"She isn't going."

"What do you mean — 'she isn't going.' Of course she is."

"She's changed her mind."

Very flatly Stan said, "I haven't changed mine."

Mark's smile turned to a brittle, black stare. "Do you reckon you can stop me, Stan?"

Stan's answer was quick and harsh. "You know damned well I can."

Instead of exploding, the two-gun man suddenly threw back his head in that white-toothed way he had, and laughed. "Stan — you damned old woman — you wouldn't say anything if I was going to marry her."

"No, but you aren't. Mark, I know you."

"The hell I'm not! I'm going to marry her right now — tonight!"

Stan's blue eyes swung to CarrieLee with a surprised look in them. He even smiled a little, crookedly. "He's luckier'n he deserves, ma'm," he said.

She didn't speak. Events had crowded up into a swift, snarled undertow that was pulling her this way and that. It was a fitting climax, in a way, that the entire wonderful day should end like this. She was breathing heavily and standing motionless with a lustre in her grey eyes.

Mark moved closer, drew her to him and kissed her ardently. Her instinctive response was fervent. Stan let out a long pent-up breath and moved aimlessly around the room. When they broke apart there was a sad light in his face.

"I've been waiting for that to happen to me for twenty-five years," he said in a dry, half-joking way, "and it hasn't happened yet. But Mark finds it in five hours in Abilene." He gave a little shrug. "Well — let's go hunt the parson."

"You go get him," Mark said with a wide smile.

Stan shook his head. "Nope. We'll *all* go, pardner. Like I said — I know you, Mark."

They all went out into the crisp spring night and they all went to the parson's house together. The cleric was dubious. Mark never could have convinced him either, and CarrieLee with the shine in her eyes and the hot blood under her face didn't try. Stan made it sound very ordinary though, so the minister married them, and until they were back out in the chilly night again, CarrieLee didn't get the full import — then she did and her first reaction was one of fright.

"What'll dad say?"

Mark laughed softly. "He won't be any trouble, honey. I'll handle him." He shot Stan a glowering, triumphant look. "Or maybe Stan'll go sit with him tonight and sort of explain things."

Stan said nothing. It was clearly his destiny this night, to leave them alone. Bedding down with the drunken old trapper, however, held no allure. He was still debating his own course when they got back to the rickety stairway, and there Mark stepped between Stan and the dingy lift and wagged his head with an ironic twinkle in his black eyes.

"See you in a day or two, Stan."

"Well — we could have a stirrup-cup," Stan said in a aggrieved way. "That's what you do on your wedding night."

"Like hell, pardner," the two-gun man said. "You've already made me wait like a corralled stud-horse. You just go roll in at the liverybarn loft — and I hope you get barley beards in your underwear."

With that, Mark turned and led CarrieLee up the long, dark stairway.

Stan was lost. It wasn't just the bed, it was a lot of things. Like walking through a boisterous town with a big slug of loneliness eating away inside him. There was something sort of like a personal loss, too, because

34

CarrieLee reminded him of another girl a long way off. The memory stabbed him, drove pain up through him like a hot iron.

He went into a saloon and bought a drink. Horse-thieves have feelings, too, he thought, watching the moving crowd of flushed, greasy faces with their whisky pallor up around the eyes. Even horsethieves like Stan Stryker was.

He downed the drink. But what the hell, it made him feel good about Mark — only he knew him pretty well, too. Still — you couldn't ever tell. If he didn't settle down with her, then he was as crazy as they came. She was something you heard about but didn't often see; an honest-to-God country girl. Clean as a sound colt and prettier than any damned back bar painting in a saloon ever was.

He thought of the old man. Of Tim. It made his mouth quirk up at the outer edges. A dry, hard smile; mirthless. Damned old fossil deserved no better than he got. The more he thought about it the more it amused him in a sterile way. In that morbid frame of mind he bought a bottle from a lemon-faced barkeep who had a knack of never looking up when he served people, and walked out of the saloon with it. He'd awaken old Tim and they'd get good and drunk together. He'd also — in his own good time — tell Tim what had happened.

Outside, he paused and looked up at the cobalt sky. Into the dark places where the stars weren't. So there was a God up there, was there? Where?

★ ★ ★

Tim Dolan went back to the cabin on Hungry Creek alone. He drove back like he had driven out, hunched over, a cud of chewing tobacco under one grey cheek, his eyes sunken, listless, seeing without sight.

He reopened his old cabin when the heat was almost a weight on the land. A heavy, constant drug that sucked away the energy of man and animal alike. It was middle summer. The beauty, the richness, the blessedness of spring was gone. In its place was the brassy, hurting heat, and when Forge Windsor returned with the Pothook crew, driving calfy-cows out of Texas, he rode over. Tim told him the story from the shade of the east side of the cabin.

"Damn you," Forge roared. "You're lying. She wouldn't have."

"I'm tellin ye the gospel truth, boy. She's got her share o' town finery now. She's a lady an' maybe it was always meant t'be. She wasn't a prairie woman. Ye could see . . ."

Forge reached down blindly with a terrible fury in his heart where the agony was the deepest, and wrenched Tim Dolan off the bench and shook him with one powerful arm, then flung him away. Afterwards, he mounted his horse and rode out into the pitiless sun, aimlessly.

There was no purpose to the way he rode. First, toward Fontaine, then he swung around and went toward Pothook, then he veered off at the last moment and rode steadily towards the sagebrush hills, and finally he got down and led his horse, hour after hour, through the hush and closeness of a long, black night.

He moved with the furious stride of a tormented man. As though, through the spending of his energy, he might kill the wretchedness of despair.

By the time he came to his brother's homestead in the foothills overlooking the eternal prairie, he had blisters, blood-shot eyes, and a feverish hollowness in his heart. He arrived in the cool, grey dawn. Just in time to see his brother raise up with a startled look from the little pile of firewood he was gathering for the cookstove.

They faced one another across the clearing. Luther Windsor was taller than Forge, five years older, less energetic-looking but with the same wide shoulders, narrow hips and bulging muscles. His eyes were blue and thoughtful and gentle-looking. He stared at Forge as though the younger man was an apparition.

"What's the matter, Forge?" A sinking sensation was in Luther. "You look — bad. Like you're in — trouble."

Forge led his horse in closer, offsaddled, unbridled, dumped the paraphernalia on the ground and dropped down on the chopping block. He was grey. Grey in the face, greyer in the heart and soul. He slumped, the wildness burned low. Only the embers showed in his eyes; the dregs and the bitterness. He didn't speak. Luther went closer, his dark reddish hair thick and unruly. He had only just gotten up. It was very early. He looked with concern at Forge, then dropped to one knee in front of the younger man.

"You didn't kill somebody, did you?"

"Kill 'em?" Forge said harshly. "No. Why would I want to kill 'em?"

"What is it then?"

"I'm a damned fool, is all." Forge's glance lifted to his brother's face. "A total damned fool. You ever find out you were all wrong — through and through — about everything — all at once?"

"No," Luther said slowly, puzzled but patient. "No — I never have." Then he settled a little and waited.

"I did. I was wrong, Lute. Wrong as all get-out." Forge straightened a little on the stump. "I figured a man'd do well to get a few head and a place to run 'em. I always figured a man'd get there someday, if he worked hard."

"That's right," Luther said placidly.

"No it isn't," Forge threw back at him in sudden violence. "You're wrong as hell, too, Lute. Only a fool will sweat like you do and like I have done. What counts is money. Not achievement, Lute — money. You got to get it and lots of it, but not with your hands. That's too slow. No sir. You get money and make *it* work for you, unless you're a damned fool like I've been. Like you are, grubbing with your hands clearing stump land, chaining out sage. It's all wrong, Lute. Listen — when you get money you can buy anything you want. Houses with wooden floors, fancy clothes — anything."

"Well, almost anything, I reckon," Lute said.

Forge shot him a savage look. "Anything, I said. The best horses, the best land, houses, women — anything under the sun."

"Not my kind of women," Luther said quietly, watching the fire rekindle itself in his brother's face.

"You're a fool, too," Forge said angrily. "Any kind of women, Lute."

Luther's gaze grew thoughtful. He hunkered there in silence watching Forge for a moment, then he spoke as quietly as before. "One of us is a fool, Forge. I'm not sure which, but I don't think it's me. How about Ma, Forge — how about Marge?"

Forge's look grew troubled. "Ma was different," he said finally. "And your wife, too." He twisted a little on the chopping block. "That's how I got fooled, Lute. Mind you — she made a damned fool out of me; no woman'll ever do that again. No sir. I had Ma's memory in me — well — I found out they aren't all the same. Most of 'em are as rotten as rattlesnakes. The prettier they are the rottener they are." He swung back to face his brother. Luther was watching him with deep concern. There were only the two of them. It had been like that for six years. Since the pneumonia epidemic of 1850.

"Lute; they'll sell out everything, for city clothes and wooden floors. All right. I've learned two things. Sweat won't get you anywhere, is one thing. The other is, money. Lots of money. That's what they worship. That's what the whole damned world worships. Then I reckon we'd best get all of it we can. From now on that's all I want. Money — heaps of it. Lute, you watch — I'll get it, too."

"Yeah," Luther said looking down at the chips around the chopping block. "It's good stuff but it isn't as easy to get as you think it is. I know." There was a gentle wryness in Luther's face.

"The hell it isn't, Lute. I'll get it. We'll get it together, if you want to ride along."

Luther grinned for the first time. His patient glance with rueful humour in it clung to Forge's face. "How? Just how're we going to get all this money?"

Forge's hot glance stayed unwaveringly on his brother's face. "Are you willing to throw in with me, Lute?"

"I reckon." That time Luther laughed. "Any time there's a way to make money — honestly, mind you — I'm for it. What have you got in mind?"

"Your homestead here, to start with." Forge watched the humour stifle itself quickly in Luther's features. "I'll help you, Lute. We'll get another team and I'll help you finish clearing off the sage. We'll clean up the place, trim those shade trees around the house so next summer they'll be prettier. We'll keep your cattle off the green feed until it's well up, then we'll throw 'em in and when they're tallow-fat, we'll go down to Fontaine and offer your place up for sale."

"How long — where did you get that idea, Forge?"

"I got it last night. I want money, Lute. So much I can make people step soft around me. I've got to have a start. Your claim is it."

Luther listened and formed words on his lips. Forge brushed them aside with a slashing gesture of his arm. His blue eyes were sparkling with cold intensity.

"We'll sell her high, Lute. As high as we can. After that we'll get more land and do it all over again. Cheap land's all there is for fellers like us to make money off of. Settlers keep coming. We've got no money to start

40

with, Lute, so we've got to use the cheapest, fastest thing around to start out with. That's your claim. Lute — land's the fastest selling thing on the frontier and you know it."

Luther moved his legs. They were getting cramped. He crossed them Indian fashion under him and felt around for his tobacco sack. Forge waited, watched the smoke drift lazily upwards in the wonderful coolness and watched his brother's face, too.

Luther ran a calloused hand through his wealth of bronze-coloured hair. He smoked and frowned and Forge waited, finally making a cigarette of his own to occupy his hands, and looked out over the sheen of golden prairie that lay like an ocean of grass, as far as he could see, down and away from the sagebrush uplands.

His glance went down to the meandering little watershed known as Hungry Creek. Followed it over each twist and turn with the writhings of his soul keeping pace, until he came down where Tim Dolan's cabin would be, then he inhaled deeply and flung his glance away in a big, aimless circle, and brought it back to Luther's face.

"Well?"

Luther shook his head in a dogged way. "Forge; this is our home, Marge likes it here. It's cool in the summer. We've got good water."

"Those are the things that'll fetch a good price, Lute," Forge said mercilessly. "If she likes it so'll some other woman. After you sell it you can buy her a place five times as nice with the extra money."

41

They talked — argued — until the sun was overhead. Neither had a sense of time. A stirring idea was between them. A way to make money. They discussed it and threshed it over and were near agreement by the time Luther's wife, wondering, a little annoyed, looked out of the door of the cabin and saw young Forge talking to her husband with a fierce intentness she'd never seen in him before.

"Lute? Bring me some kindling and I'll build the fire."

It startled both of them. Forge looked over at his sister-in-law as though she were a stranger. She saw the look and said, "Hello, Forge. Whatever you two are hatching must be very important. Lute forgot to fire up the stove." She was smiling at them. Forge smiled back — with his mouth; she was a woman.

Luther got up, dusted his britches and looked at his wife with a drawn smile. The thoughts in his head were still of money. "I'll fetch it," he said. "Come on, Forge."

They took in the wood and said very little until they had eaten, then they both went back outside and Forge hammered home his points while Luther fed his horses, then they went into the shade and talked almost all the rest of the morning.

In the afternoon, they started to work.

Forge quit the Pothook. He took his pay and bought another team of big, solid, sound horses. They worked almost grimly, rarely talking about anything but their labour and their plans. Luther's wife pieced it together and had a woman's usual balkiness towards change, but by then Luther was convinced.

They were burnt black by the sun and dropped like logs at the end of the day. Their horses grew lean from work, and hard. As hard and powerful as the resolve that drove Forge night and day.

It took the balance of the summer and all that winter, but by the following spring Luther's ranch was a picture. When the feed was high they turned Lute's cattle in on it and that *was* a picture; tall, lush feed, fattening cattle . . .

"It's time to drive into Fontaine," Forge said, the evening they were leaning over the pasture rails watching the newborn calves. Luther heaved a mighty sigh and fell into a long silence that he didn't break for a long time.

"Just when it's a real ranch, Forge."

Forge swore softly. "That's just it, Lute. That's what we've been sweating for. If you fall in love with it all over again, so'll the next feller. Let's go down in the morning."

They went. The result of their trip was a very profitable sale, too, and until Marge saw the stacks of money, she protested, but she grew thoughtfully silent afterward, and Forge noticed the change with a vicious look in his eyes.

Luther bought two brand new wagons. He took Marge to Fontaine, then later, all the way to Abilene. He bought her clothes and such happiness as she'd never known before in her life.

Forge didn't want to go with them. He was downright stubborn about it. So, while they spent a little on a deserved holiday, he bought three splendid saddlehorses and rode out from Fontaine's land office to the rolling hill land, and back, looking for cheap, raw land that could be developed fast, inexpensively, and profitably.

By the time Luther and Marge came home Forge had found what he wanted. Two adjoining pieces that a minimum of clearing would make into a sizable cow ranch. He sat in the hotel in Fontaine with his hat on the back of his head, listening to Marge's talk. Luther sat back in the evening shadows studying his younger brother's face. Seeing the restlessness, the burning zeal and the resolve there, stronger than ever. He sighed inwardly. Forge was going to sweat both of them down again.

While his wife talked and Forge listened with polite smiles and growing impatience, Luther thought of their bank balance. It was a sobering, extremely pleasant reflection. He finally interrupted Marge, who took the cue and left them alone. There were still people in Fontaine she hadn't told everything to.

Left alone, the brothers hitched their chairs closer. Luther produced a bottle of Irish whiskey and some cigars he'd brought back from Abilene. His calm eyes searched Forge's face as the younger man lit up.

"Well, Forge? What've you got this time?"

"A bigger chunk, Lute. It'll take work but we'll make big money off it, too."

"Prairie land?"

"Nope. Up in the sagebrush sea again. Prairie land's too risky. The big cowmen'd fight us. We're after money, not a war."

44

Luther poured off two shots of whiskey, shoved one towards Forge and took one himself. He leaned back and looked out the window into the drifting dusk. The mellowest of memories went across his mind's eye. He was a solid, placid, inward man, with a gentleness to him that was in contrast to Forge's increasing restlessness of spirit. A warmth worked inside his head, with the fumes of the Irish whiskey rising, and he wondered if he should mention seeing CarrieLee over at Abilene. No; someday maybe — if Forge ever brought her up again, but not now, anyway. He swung back and watched his brother drain off the whiskey and draw upon his cigar.

"Did you buy the land, Forge?"

"Yep. Got the patents at the land office, in the safe. It's all clear land." Forge's blue eyes, with the taint of pain in their backgrounds, were wide and appraising. "I figure the brushing-off and stocking will be my job, Lute. We'll work this piece differently. You take over the house-building and development of the barns and corrals and that stuff. Make the house-area nice, sort of. Marge's your helper. She'll be able to steer you along like a woman'd want things." He grinned. "You're cut out for making homes, you two. Me — I'm the other kind, Lute."

Luther smiled. "Man of the sagebrush sea, eh?" He finished off his whiskey. "That sounds all right. When do you reckon we ought to start?"

"No hurry," Forge said, arising, still wearing his cruel little smile. "Tomorrow morning's soon enough." Then he laughed.

Luther got up too, turning his empty glass in his fist. He was smiling a little. "You'll work us to death," he said.

"No; to riches, Lute, not to death. I'll be around in the morning to get you. Leave Marge here at the hotel for a few days. We won't need that woman's touch yet a while."

Luther nodded in silence. He watched Forge leave the room and stood thoughtfully thinking about his brother, then he turned and crossed to the window, looked out and down on the dusty little town. The land lay with a benediction of heavy restfulness on it.

He watched Forge walk to his handsome, big bay horse, untie, swing up and wheel away. Until that moment he hadn't thought to ask Forge where he was staying, but he found out the following day when they went to the new land together.

Forge had a canvassed-over Studebaker wagon. He lived in it. There were also three other camps for men on the new ranch. Forge pointed out those were where their hired hands lived, and Luther's surprise was complete.

"Hired men? I thought we were going to do this developing ourselves, like before."

Forge shook his head sharply. "Not the sweaty work, Lute. We're the brains and we hire the brawn. Don't worry though, old horse, there'll be plenty of sweating for both of us, but not like before. Now, we're bosses. We get some of the sweat and all of the headaches."

He looked at his older brother and laughed as they sat in the warm sun on their horses, watching the labourers at the chore of clearing brush. "The Windsor brothers are moving now, Lute. We're on our way to that money I told you about."

And they were, but the big ranch took them months and months of the hardest kind of work before it was ready. New-looking, fresh and thriving from every angle, presentable to whoever could afford it, for it was a staggeringly expensive outfit.

Moreover, they had to co-operate with the seasons. That held them over for another year so the feed would be green and tall again when they turned their growing herds in upon it. Like before, which was a pure coincidence, Forge came striding through the dusk and leaned on the pole fence where Luther was smoking in peace and quiet, watching the night lowering, and spoke of selling.

"Well — she's ready, Lute. You want to take a trip?"

"Trip?" Luther said, turning to face his brother. "Where?"

Forge leaned heavily on the railings. He was leaner, harder looking, with the blunt thrust of his jaw more pronounced and the flash of his blue eyes more calculating. "Hell," he said. "We can't sell *this* in Fontaine. We want too much money for it."

"Where'll we sell it then?"

"Back east. There's lots of big money outfits back there, Lute. Lots of investors who want to come west. I'm not the type for this and you are. You're — well — more a gentleman than I am. I'm the workhorse — you're the salesman. Take a couple of months, take Marge too. We'll add it to expenses and tack it on the sale price. Chicago. Cincinnati. New York, maybe. Just sort of drift around and mix where there's big money."

Luther considered his cigar ash. His heart was beating with a new cadence. Marge would love it and so would he. It was a little dizzying, a little frightening. He looked shrewdly at his brother.

"You're not the workhorse, Forge, you're the brains."

Forge half turned away as though he found the statement acceptable, but one of those things a man shouldn't say aloud. "Well — when can you leave?"

Luther threw aside his cigar. There was an understanding look on his face. When Forge asked a question like that, he meant you were to leave the first thing in the morning. "You're a slave driver, do you know that?" he said.

Forge looked up. "Well, to tell you the truth, Lute, I've got my eye on two more pieces that're right smack-dab on the emigrant trail westward. There's a lot of brush but the land's good and level. We can't move until we get our money out of this one, though. You understand?"

Luther didn't say whether he understood or not. All he did say was, "I'll be damned." He was going to say more, but he didn't, not for a long time, then it wasn't what he'd been thinking at all.

"All right, Forge. I'll see when Marge can be ready."

"Good. And something I've had in my craw for a while, Lute. This next place — we'll work it a little different. We'll let it pay off in cattle for a year or two before we cash in. All right?"

48

Luther was hoping against hope that the thought behind Forge's remark was an urge to settle down. Luther liked the profits fine; he was also a little weary, but mainly, he lacked Forge's blind-stubborn drive. Forge's next remark blasted his hope.

"Well — on the emigrant trail there'll be a good chance we can build up a fat cattle, horses, mules and oxen trade. We'd make money both ways, you see. On the land and on the emigrants." The motionless blue eyes were like the sun off a snowfield. "We want a lot of money, Lute; remember?"

"Yeh. Good night, Forge." But Luther didn't move right away even though he started to. "You know, Forge," he said, "a man could stay right here on this place and do real good. Cattle're making money now."

Forge shook his head. The stubborn jaw was limned in the deepening shadows. "Too damned slow, Lute. We want fast profits and lots of money." He didn't wait for Luther to speak again, but turned on his heel and strode off. Luther watched him go. The same bleak restlessness was as strong in him as ever.

Lute and Marge went east. They spent money because they had it to spend. They moved where the money was and acquired the graces that went with the atmosphere and environment they moved in.

They sold the big ranch at a staggering profit and returned to Fontaine with the news and the money. They found Forge leaner, older looking, his eyes perpetually squinted against the blasting sunlight, working like their commonest labourer, developing new land. He stopped long enough to appraise them both

49

with the sweat running darkly under his faded shirt, and make a low, mocking bow at their elegance.

"She's sold, Forge," Luther told him.

There was a quick, almost impatient nod. "Sure. I knew you'd do it. We're a good team, Lute. The best in the west."

Marge's eyes were steady on Forge's face. "You're working too hard. Lord; you must have lost thirty pounds. Forge — you'd better move into Fon . . ."

"All I need's a little of your cooking, Marge." He swung with a raised arm and pointed towards a secluded, tree-shaded knoll. "How'll that be for the house area? If you like it we'll start brushing it off tomorrow. That's all I've been waiting for, Marge. What do you say?"

"It's a lovely spot," she said warmly, watching Forge's face with a strange look in her eyes.

Luther was a little heavier around the middle. He stood wide-legged, saying nothing, just looking. Forge's eyes crinkled. "You show up tomorrow, old moneybags," he said. "I'll get that tallow off you."

Luther smiled absently, eyeing Forge objectively, then he said, "Maybe I could give you a few pounds, Forge. Like Marge said . . ."

"I never heard of work killing anyone," Forge said shortly. He left them after that.

On the drive back to the hotel in Fontaine Luther seemed withdrawn, occupied with his thoughts. When Marge spoke he turned owlishly and looked at her.

"I don't imagine he'll work himself to death," she said, "but he's surely burning himself out — this way."

"No," Luther said slowly. "I never heard of anyone working themselves to death either. But I'm not sure that's what kills men that drop in the harness, either."

"What do you mean?"

Luther fiddled with the driving lines before he answered. "Something inside them. Whatever it is that drives them day and night like Forge is being driven. I reckon that's what kills 'em, Marge — not the sweat."

She said nothing.

CHAPTER
THREE

Discord from the Anvil Grows . . .

Back in Abilene before the first year died, CarrieLee had her recurrent queasiness. It had been bad shortly after her marriage to Mark Belleau. So bad, in fact, that she was weak and covered with perspiration and Mark, in his alarm, had been the soul of gentleness — for a while. For a short while. Just long enough for an awful truth to burst inside his brain. Then he left her alone for three days. Had, in fact, hunted up Stan and gone out with him into the blackest night.

CarrieLee was ill and well by spells, but she was neither, so much as baffled, when Mark came back. His dark, liquid eyes were haggard, blacker than she had ever seen them. He was mud-splattered and impassive. The gentleness was gone except in rare fits when he was solicitous. Once, like that, she asked him what her strange malady could be, and he had regarded her steadily for a long time, lighted a cigar and sucked on it with an unblinking stare, before he spoke.

"Sickness? No, it isn't that." He had broken off into a fit of wild cursing. She watched him, more perplexed

52

than ever, then he checked himself and made a bitter smile that his smouldering eyes didn't enhance any.

"My little unsoiled dove from far off Fontaine. My little trapper's daughter from a wilderness log cabin. My little wife who has caught Mark Belleau with a wedding band so she'll have a name for her child!"

He left her alone again, after that, and it was as well, for, while the sting of his words cut her, she was vastly curious whether what he said was true or not. It was. She found that out later from the doctor in Abilene.

She also found out that a man has more than one side to his nature. Mark wasn't abusive so much as he was cruel in a refined way. He slept alone, rarely came to see her while they lived at the hotel, and he rode out with Stan Stryker more and more, so that while there was always plenty of money — she knew not from where — the days were more agonising in their loneliness than Hungry Creek and her father's cabin had ever been.

With the fantastic ebb and flow of the most lavish displays of wealth and the most abject shows of poverty, the frontier parted and flowed on both sides of her. She had no friends in Abilene although there was plenty to see. There was nothing to do and no place for an unescorted girl to go. It was like being imprisoned in a world peopled by multitudes that you could see and hear — but never get close to. She drew more and more apart, lived within herself, created a pathetic little world of her own, and waited.

During the long, wearying months, Stan came to see her. She had always liked him. Still did. He was kind and understanding, or at least he gave that impression, so she asked him to come often. He did — as often as his work didn't take him out of town.

And Mark tried. Be it to his credit, he tried. Twice he came back muddy, tired to death and hollow-eyed, and took her out on the town. Both times he got so drunk she had to send for Stan, and between them they got him back to the hotel. After that he didn't turn up for several weeks. The uncertainty was showing on her, too. So much so, in fact, that when Stan came back one time in the dead of night, she almost cried out in relief from her loneliness upon recognising his voice. They were terrible days growing darker, like the light within her was growing darker, being extinguished by slow degrees.

When her child was born it was a girl. A blue-eyed girl with even, cameo features. She was absorbed in it. The brightness came into her days a little. It grew as did her daughter. Stronger, sturdier, so that Mark's strangeness became less of a torment in her mind. A thing to be endured but shuntled far back behind this magic of new life that had come from her.

"What'll you name her?"

CarrieLee looked into the jet black eyes and longed for something that was no longer there. "Would you like Maria? It's as close as I can get to Mark."

That was when she first saw the depth of hatred in him. It had stared out at her with burning intensity for a moment, before he swung up and stomped out of the room.

54

He was gone twelve days that time, and during those long, blustery fall days, CarrieLee came to recognise more and more of Forge Windsor in her daughter. It thrilled her. She even smiled a little and laughed, playing with Maria. Then Stan came.

It was before dawn with the stark, leaden sky showing through the naked limbs of the trees and the stilled breath of frost in the air. He knocked on the door and moved in quickly when she opened it. She was stunned at his appearance. His face was pale with an unhealthy sweat on it. The blue eyes, always steady, were feverish with an awful restlessness. His clothing was layered with dust and old sweat, his hands were scratched from intimate contact with sage and spiney brush. His smile was gone as though it never had existed, and he spoke with his hand outstretched, offering her a heavy little bag.

"CarrieLee — here. You'll need this. That's all you'll ever get. Mark is dead. That's his money."

She didn't take the little pouch so Stan tossed it across the room on the bed and his eyes were snagged by Maria's crib. They dropped with a raw bleakness to the child's sleeping form and stayed there a moment then came back to CarrieLee's face. It was white, blanched, frozen with an appalled look of horror and shock.

"We moved in on a herd I'd studied out. There was a posse waiting." He shrugged. "Mark never had a chance. He was half drunk anyway. One of them shot him with a rifle. He never knew what hit him. I got him cleaned out before they caught up. That's the money."

He stopped, breathing heavily, looking down into her face with something she'd never seen in *his* eyes before. Coldness; almost repugnance.

He shook his head just the tiniest bit at her. "I've been pitying myself all this time because he was so lucky. Lord!" He felt for the door-latch with one hand and looked back at her. "Well, there's more'n enough money in his pouch for both of you, but make it last, CarrieLee. Adios."

He was gone like he had come, grimy, cat-footed, his big gun swaying with his stride, moving out under the sick, grey sky and into the wintery gusts that tore out of somewhere and gnawed at Abilene. That was all the good-byes there were. Mark dead in disgrace and her slowly awakened understanding that he had been an outlaw all the time.

And Stan's final contempt, which had been the worst of all to bear. Mark — she had become adjusted to his scorn, his deep-writhing hatred, but Stan had always seemed so solid to her, so friendly and gentle and understanding. And the worse-than-ever loneliness now.

Those were the good-byes to all that had been and if it hadn't been for Maria she would have stayed longer in her stunned stupor, her anguished daze and shock, but the young have bellies, and empty, they are especially articulate about re-filling. So, from her daughter came the resurgent will to live and surmount, for with Maria now, she had to think ahead. Consider the future.

Abilene had another rash of its seasonal bursting at the seams the spring following Mark's death, and Stan Stryker's disappearance. The flow of people from the east was amazing. They came any way they could, but mostly with huge wagons and gentle-eyed oxen yoked to them. Some came a-horseback, proud and travelling fast. Others came tooling farm wagons or little Red River carts.

CarrieLee watched it all with just a shading of her old thrill revived for a time. Then she saw the illnesses the wretched stragglers brought, and that frightened her for Maria's sake. She stood "up in the air," as Mark had once called it, and gazed out over the spring-drenched prairies westward.

Nostalgia brought back vivid memories of Fontaine, her father, Hungry Creek. The golden days she had known. All closed doors to her now.

But there would be other places just as pleasant, for each year new towns were arising. Sturdy little towns where people planted trees the first thing. The farther west the Indians were pushed, the closer civilisation followed with its villages and cleared-over land. She held her daughter and rocked her in the gloaming with the fever of adventure — of another spring — in her eyes. Good-bye Abilene . . .

She went west with a large emigrant train. A solitary woman travelling alone was looked askance at, but not a widow-woman with a blue-eyed daughter like Maria. CarrieLee made friends almost as fast as her daughter did, and shortly she had a place among the pioneers.

In fact, the men of the train came often to her little cooking-fire because she, alone among them, knew the land ahead. As far as Fontaine anyway. Then there was widower Asa Knowlton, a wealthy man with two spindly sons, who was seeking a place in the sun where his boys might grow to manhood with the strength in them that nature hadn't seen fit to endow them with through inheritance, and that was odd, too, for Asa Knowlton was a bull of a man.

Unimaginative, a little inclined towards taciturnity perhaps, but strong as an ox and with considerable wealth, although few knew this, including CarrieLee, until he told her; Asa was a stolid, earthy man.

He came often. Asa Junior and William, aged nine and eleven, with their too-large eyes full of childish bewilderment and solemnity, touched her. Nearly nineteen, CarrieLee was in all ways a woman. Asa saw this, was moved by it in an age-old way, and very methodically, with monumental patience, laid siege to her heart. But never openly, he was too wise a business-man for that, knowing as he did that he himself was no find for a young woman with a sparkling youth and what he suspected was an embittered heart as well. Still, in his own silent way, Asa worked at the undertaking very painstakingly, and by the time the wagon-train made the town of Sageland, he and CarrieLee both knew what his objective was.

Sageland was a wide place in the westward passage. A town some visionary had encouraged to grow in the narrow slot of land between the sagebrushed hills and the flat endlessness of the prairie. It had the hurrying air of all such places and the ring of the anvils in smithies was a constant reminder that time was fleeing, that horses needed shoeing and wagon tyres needed shrinking against the heat ahead, if those who were set with their faces towards the setting sun were to keep their rendezvous with destiny.

CarrieLee saw its raw newness from her cart. Around the bulk of Asa Knowlton, she could see the people, too, and once she jerked up her team so sharply one of the horses reared. Asa looked down at her with a little frown of disapproval.

"What is it, CarrieLee? A dog run in front of you?"

Her face was white and the grey eyes were large and she was slow to answer. "No — not a dog, Asa."

"Well, let's get on then. The folks'll want to camp just beyond town I expect."

But she didn't move for a long time, and even when she did the long stride of a bronzed man was vivid in her mind. Forge Windsor! Forge Windsor here — in this little frontier town! It couldn't be but it was. She'd know him anywhere. The clean sweep of his profile, the colour of his hair, thick always and a little unruly — wild even. The way he walked and looked — she'd know all those things to her dying day.

But Sageland was eighty miles north and at least that far west of old Fontaine. The Pothook wouldn't be running cattle up this far. Oh, but things would have changed since then. She kept forgetting the years that had slid by. Forge might be anywhere. There were the years . . .

The next day, while Asa and some other men were in Sageland soberly studying the fresh oxen and strong horses for sale or trade, she found a man who would go seeking Forge. It didn't cost her any more than the price of a few drinks in the green-planking saloon, either. Then came the waiting, out at the emigrant camp, which was the worst. And the doubting. Then, when the man came back with his breath preceding him like an invisible fog, he verified that it *was* Forge Windsor. Not only Forge Windsor, but *Mister* Forge Windsor.

"In the saloons they say he's the richest man around. Owns nigh the whole town and the land aroun' it. Pretty cussed rich man. Got over two thousan' head of critters an' they say him and his brother's got a ranch-house that's made of real planed-wood with furniture from way back east."

He had an office too, she learned, and that stayed in her mind when the rest of it was vague, like a dream that lacked the courage of reality.

It wasn't hard to get Maria taken care of for a while. Then she scrubbed herself like she had in the golden days, dressed in her finest with a huge and handsome bow behind her at the hips, and went into Sageland.

She went slowly, missing very little, from the smells of green wood and freshly cut hay, to the odours of the cattle pens and high, pole horse corrals. The full import of what her informer had said didn't soak in until she saw the brand on the penned animals. W. & W. Windsor and Windsor. Forge and his brother.

She walked carefully, for the duckboards were new and the heat had shrunk them, leaving gaps that trapped the unwary between the boards. She tried to recollect Forge's brother. She couldn't; hadn't seen him more than three or four times that she knew of, and in those days Luther had been just another slab-sided squatter with a brush-ranch who had a tired, overworked looking little drab of a wife.

A glaringly reflected glass window caught her attention. She turned and read the names. Windsor & Windsor. Land, Cattle, Horses & Equipment. She smiled to herself. It wasn't like Forge at all; he must have changed considerably. She entered the office and was stopped by a smooth-faced man about her own age.

"Ma'am?" he said.

"I'd like to see Mister Windsor."

"Which one? There are two of them — ma'am."

"Mister Forge Windsor."

He got up and kept his eyes on her face while he got her a chair. "I'll see if he's in yet."

She sat, looking at the desk and shelves of scattered, much-handled maps rolled carelessly. Smelt the cigar mustiness of the place and was filled with an overpowering curiosity about this new Forge Windsor. None of what she saw belonged to the Forge Windsor she had known — the Pothook rider with the will to struggle and labour and sweat in the prairie air.

While she waited the clerk went into Forge's office and waited respectfully. "There's a lady out front that wants to see you, Sir."

Forge glanced up briefly. "What's her name?" he asked, wondering who it was.

The clerk reddened. "I — forgot to ask, Sir."

Forge's blue eyes lingered, with their hardness. "Well; you'd better find out," he said, and dropped his glance again.

The young man went back to CarrieLee and asked her name. He was flustered but CarrieLee didn't notice it because the problem of her name was suddenly, painfully, brought to mind. Forge wouldn't know any Mrs. Belleau. Very slowly she said, "Tell him Miss CarrieLee Dolan."

The clerk took it back and spoke it into the suddenly hushed atmosphere of Forge's office. His answer was bitingly, very clearly, thrown back.

"Tell her I'm not here."

"But Sir — she knows I've talked to you."

"I don't give a damn what she knows, Tom. Tell her I'm not here. Do you understand?"

"Yes sir."

The clerk went out and closed the door gently, but very firmly, behind him. Forge felt a sudden urge to get up from his desk. He did; went to a glass jar and took out a cigar, bit it viciously, lit it, and exhaled through a rush of bitterness that seemed to have come up within recent seconds to line the inside of his mouth.

He crossed to a window and stared out of it. The smoke wreathed his head. Beyond the window was Sageland. Men swarmed. New buildings were going up. Traders were hunkered around, down by his trading corrals. Freighters cursed robustly at their hitches, trying to back up to the unloading docks with loads of hardware — his. The sounds of anvils were bell-like. That was a sound that, to Forge, was the heartbeat of his town. He loved the sound — or had up to now. Now there was a harsh note of discord to their tones.

Everywhere was what he had created — thanks to a lesson *she* had taught him. Sageland was money and he, Forge Windsor, was Sageland. He and Luther, but he had no illusions there, either. Lute had softened up a lot in the last two years. He and Marge had their phaeton, their matched chestnut driving team, their entertainments.

Forge removed the cigar from beneath his teeth and clamped them down so that his jaw muscles rippled. Lute and Marge had what they wanted and he had what he wanted — money. He turned sharply away from the window —

She was standing in the doorway looking at him.

"I said I didn't want to see you." The words were cold and bleak.

She didn't answer him nor move. He held the cigar in fingers that were taut, oily-slick and trembling a little. CarrieLee! God; why did you let her come back like this after all this time! The white line that was knife-edge thin above his upper lip was there for her to see and recall. The blackness of his expression and the iciness of his eyes were things she had never seen before.

"You've changed," she said finally. "You've changed a lot, Forge."

"It hasn't been the original two months," he said bitterly.

"You remember that, don't you?"

He threw his answer at her like it was a curse. "If God would have let me forget, I'd of gladly done it. And you — and all like you. I'd of forgotten a long time ago."

"God won't," she said, "and neither will I."

"No, you'd like to think it's always around to pain me, wouldn't you? Do you treat your husband like that, too?"

"He's dead."

"He's fortunate then," Forge said with strength and great cruelty.

She didn't feel any pain, right away, at what he said. She was too absorbed in looking at him. His eyes have changed, she thought, and his mouth. The stubbornness is all there in his face; the terrific drive that used to scare me. Oh — he's terribly changed. There's no tenderness left in him. He was finding understanding in those days. That's all gone out of him now.

"I made him as happy as I could, Forge."

"I'm sure of it. And now he's dead." The hateful sarcasm dripped from every word. "I'm lucky you didn't try to make me happy."

"I *did* try — you know I did. I've never tried as hard since."

"But two months was just too long to wait, wasn't it? I'm glad, CarrieLee. You didn't have the guts for what it would have taken to stay with me through the hard work. I'm gladder it didn't work out, than I am — of anything else I know of!"

"Forge — don't. I was too young. Try to understand. I was a child, really. I didn't know — anything."

"Didn't you?" he said savagely. "You knew you wanted a house with wooden floors and city clothes. You wanted to live where there were lots of people — in a town. You knew those things and you got them. *That's* how much of a child you were."

There was a thick vein in the side of his neck. It throbbed with a slugging, angry pulse.

"You wanted money, that's all you ever wanted, CarrieLee. Well — I've got money now; enough to buy you all the damned ostrich feathers and yellow-wheeled buggies you could ever drive." He paused and seemed to draw a new store of venom from his exultation. "So your husband died and you came hunting me again. You'd heard, maybe, that I wasn't a poor Pothook rider any more."

"Forge!"

He saw her moving, leaning against the doorway with her grey eyes the stark colour of those cloud-shadows they used to watch from their secret place at Hungry Creek. He turned a little so the shadows of the room hid his eyes from her. The memories were flooding in the background of them. The fragrance of her always, the look she'd worn that first time when she'd stared him down, the last time they'd been together. Memories steeped in soul-wringing anguish that he didn't want her to see.

"Why don't you go," he said hoarsely. "Go somewhere else to hunt."

She didn't move away from the door but she looked almost frail, leaning there. She said, "Forge!" Once more, and that was all.

He cleared his throat, remembered the cigar, put it between his teeth, found it cold and dead and flung it aside, then asked a question of her.

"Have you seen Tim lately?"

The soft, cold way he said it was like a premonition in itself. She felt the touch of unseen fingers. Cold ones. "No. I haven't seen dad in almost two years. I plan to drive down to Hungry Creek, though."

"Do you? Well — when you get near the old cabin you'll see a grave at the edge of the willows. Say hello to him for me, CarrieLee. I'm the one who put him there."

She had the hand behind her holding onto the doorjam. The fingers strained and bit deeply into the wood until the splinters stood up and gouged her flesh and drew two small drops of blood. That was the only show of feeling she made, and he didn't see that. With an effort she drew herself upright and stood perfectly still, even her eyes, looking across at him.

"Thank you for that," she said. "I — guess I'll go now. I made another mistake today, didn't I? I thought you'd be the same Forge I knew a few years ago. You're not — you're a stranger to me. A man I wouldn't want to know at all — under any circumstances."

"I'm sorry I'm a disappointment," he said with an echo to his words like a lost little breeze blowing over an old campfire where ashes lay. "If I've changed, I can thank a girl for that. A girl who couldn't even wait two months."

"I tried to tell you, Forge. I was too young. I didn't know anything. Anything at all. What happened at Abilene wasn't my doing. Ask — ," she checked herself. Her father was dead. "It doesn't matter anyway. You don't want to believe me. You can't. You're so different now from what you were, you wouldn't even try to understand. And — as far as me looking for you because you are rich, that's not so. I didn't even know where you were until yesterday afternoon when the train I'm with went through your town and I saw you walking by. But I'll tell you this because I came here expecting to find you the same. You were a wonderful person, Forge. You were something I've always remembered and always will remember. Warm and gentle and lovable. That's the part of you that's dead now. I can see that in your face. Money? I'm glad you have it, because if you didn't have it — the way you are now — you'd be unfit to be around people. It'll give you the respect it always takes with it; maybe that'll make up for what you've become."

"Is that all you have to say?" He looked older — ravaged by some inner malignancy that, in passing, had left only the husk of him behind.

"Not quite. I wish I could forget the way I've seen you this last time, but I suppose that's the part that'll live the longest. Memories usually work that way, don't they?"

She was thinking with a crystal clearness of Mark, and how her last memories of him totally overshadowed the earlier ones, when his black eyes had flashed real love at her, and the way he had of throwing back his head to laugh.

"Well — there's one way I can still see you the way you used to be. The way you used to smile and laugh, and look hurt and happy — all that. I've got an image of you, Forge."

She stopped, watching the shadows lengthen across his face. Very quietly she said, "You never knew it, Forge, but we had a daughter."

The shock moved swiftly into his eyes. It glazed them until the big vein in his neck began to throb and a dark torrent of blood boiled in under his cheeks.

"You are a liar!" he said, very softly.

"No," she said back, "I'm not lying. I don't have to lie to you because it doesn't matter whether you believe me or not. She's my reminder of the other — husband — I had. He's dead, too."

He moved a little, went over by his desk and leaned back on the top of it so that his legs had help in supporting him. Looking at her with his head back slightly, he said, "CarrieLee; do you want to know what I think? I think this was the ace-in-the-hole you intended to play when you first came in here. I think first, you planned on trying your charms. They worked once. If that failed, then you figured on trying your widowhood. Now, since that's failed too — you have this ace-in-the-hole." He lowered his head and glowered. "My daughter!" He spat it out. "Do you want to know how I know that's a lie?"

"Yes. I'd like to know that, Forge."

"Because," he was admitting something that it cost him a lot to say. "Because — I used to ride over and take a few drinks and vittals to old Tim. That's how. He kept me posted on you, and never once did he tell me you had a child. That's how!

She didn't answer him right away, but she did speak. Right when the triumph was the brightest in his bitter eyes. "Forge; I haven't seen dad since the day I was married. That's the absolute truth. You know how he was — maybe he got worse after he was alone. He rambled. He told you what you wanted to hear. Like those old stories of his Indian fights, and other things. You know better than to put faith in all that he said." She moved her head from side to side to emphasise her words. "He knew nothing of me. If you were carrying him liquor and food, he'd tell you whatever he thought would bring you back with more. I loved him and still do — he was wonderful — but I knew him very well, too, and you should have also. He knew nothing of me after he left Abilene. I did have a daughter, Forge and she is ours. Yours and mine."

He wore the stubborn jut of his jaw well forward. The bleakness in his eyes was adamant; like iron cooling after a white-hot heat. His anger was gone, almost, and in its place was the sardonic look of complete disbelief that characterised him through all the agony of their brief visit.

He said, "I don't believe you. Is that clear enough?"

"Yes," she said in a low voice, then turned and went out through the doorway and closed the panel behind her, quietly. She saw the white, still glance of the male clerk and knew he had heard every word of it, passed him as though he didn't exist, and went out into the warm, shadowing sunlight.

Forge held his arms out full length and slowly straightened out his fingers. They trembled. He said, "God damn it!" and went over to the glass humidor and lit another cigar.

The smoke was strong and foggy, but it couldn't succeed in dispelling the lingering fragrance she left behind. He went back around to his desk and gazed at the sprawling maps Luther had left there earlier, the things he had been studying when she'd come in. They gagged him now. He flung away from them and went striding into an adjoining office where Luther was sitting stone still, with his hands locked together on his desk. It startled him to see Lute sitting like that. He stopped and stared.

"What the devil's wrong with you? Don't you feel well, Lute? Are you sick?"

Luther looked up slowly. His eyes, always warm and gentle, had a heretofore never-shown coldness in their depths. A bitterness so powerful Forge was shocked, almost staggered by it. Luther spoke in his normally quiet tone of voice.

"The wall is pretty thin, Forge."

"Oh. You — heard."

70

"Yes, I heard." Luther's voice began to gather strength, and deepen. "You don't want to hear what I think — do you?"

"No!" Forge said angrily, "I don't. You had no right to eavesdrop, Lute."

"Right?" Luther said. "I had no right, Forge, you're perfectly correct. Dammit all — I had no *choice*!"

"I don't want to hear another word, Lute. Not another damned word — ever." Forge fisted his big hands and thrust them deeply into his pockets. He was leaning a little, the cigar like a challenge the way it was slanted forward in the air, matching the truculence of his blue eyes.

Luther got up slowly. "I reckon I'll go home, Forge," he said heavily.

Forge didn't speak. He watched his brother take his hat off the rack, dump it on his head and walk out in a flat-footed, old-acting way. He was still standing like that when his clerk came to Luther's doorway and looked over at him with an upset, ashen face.

"There's a man out here wants to talk about land, Mister Windsor."

His first thought was to tell the clerk to go to hell. On second thought, though, he needed this diversion. "Send him to my office," he said, turning back through the doorway.

The man who entered was big. As tall as Forge, a good fifteen years older, and a solid fifty pounds heavier. He was methodical in his movements and in his speech. He had "emigrant" written in every line of him, but more than that, he had success showing in the level, equal glance he shot at Forge when he introduced himself and offered a massive hand.

"I'm Asa Knowlton, Mister Windsor. I've been riding around your country here. I like it. Besides; farther west there's Indian trouble again. I can't see much future in investing where you may be killed any night."

Forge reacted automatically. "Have a seat, Mister Knowlton. Cigar? No? How about a little real, imported Irish whiskey?" Forge shrugged at the second refusal and sat down at his desk. "The Indians've been pushed out of here for three years now. I won't say they don't know we're here — they do — but we've never been bothered much. We're too strong for 'em now, anyway, if they get to feeling their oats. As for the land — it's for sale. That's our business, but I'll tell you this, Mister Knowlton — there isn't a better country anywhere around, for cattle and farming. I know what I'm saying. I've been in this country since I was eleven years old."

"Is that so?" Asa Knowlton said, appraising Forge's powerful shoulders. "It must be a good place to raise boys, then. You look fit enough."

"I think it's as good a place as there is for raising kids." A stab of hot pain burned into his heart. He laid aside his cigar with a curious glance at it. "How many kids have you, Mister Knowlton?"

"Two boys. Nine and eleven. I'll soon have a daughter, too, now."

"Oh," Forge said, blinking swiftly and wondering how Knowlton knew the sex beforehand. "Congratulations."

Knowlton grinned. "Well — it isn't exactly like that, I just got the promise of a widow in our train to marry me. She's got a little daughter coming three years old. Pretty as a picture."

The blue eyes on Knowlton grew round and deathly still. "A widow, Mister Knowlton? I didn't know there was one in Sageland."

"Well; she came from Abilene with our train. Name's Mrs. CarrieLee Belleau — but that's beside the point. Now — about this land —"

"Knowlton, let me interrupt you a minute. Isn't your train going on westward?"

"Yes. The destination's California, but like a lot of the others, I joined up for safety's sake. Emigrants travelling in large groups are safer than in ones and twos. I had no fixed destination in mind, though. I'm looking for a place where I can raise my children, put down roots, farm a little, run a few head of stock — you understand."

"Yes," Forge said distantly, "I understand. I understand perfectly." He thought, *so this is her way of striking back, is it? Well, it won't work.* What he said was, "Mister Knowlton, the land hereabouts is pretty expensive and, frankly, all the good pieces have either been sold already or my brother and I have reserved them."

Knowlton looked at Forge with a bewildered expression. "You just said you were in the land business, that your land was for sale. Besides, the piece I have in mind has one of your map-stakes on it. I don't believe it's been withdrawn because I looked it up.

However, if it has, there are other pieces I'm sure. The main thing is, Mister Windsor, I like this country. It has promise and seems to be just about what I've been looking for."

Forge smashed out his cigar and spoke savagely, without thought, letting the words come out the way they formed in his mind without any rearrangement. With strident harshness he said, "Mister Knowlton, the land — this damned land — isn't for sale to you at all!"

CHAPTER
FOUR

The Sagebrush Sea

Asa Knowlton was stunned. The strange wildness in Forge Windsor's stare was shocking. He sat there waiting for something — he knew not what. Rationality to return — something — but when Forge spoke again, it was with the fury leaking out of his mind via words. He leaned on his desk with a reddened face.

"Knowlton — I want you to know that there's no land around Sageland anywhere that's for sale to you!"

Then he straightened up, wrenched away his glittering stare and stalked out of the office leaving the stunned prospect to leave when he chose.

He forgot his hat and didn't see the wondering look on the clerk's face when he flung out through the roadway door and walked into the dazzling sunlight.

Sageland's hurry and bedlam enveloped him. He turned north and walked up through the lemon-coloured daylight among the hordes of people who streamed both ways. At the end of town where the new plank walkway ended abruptly, he stood gazing up into the purpling hills with their edging of silver colour, towards a large, pretentious house that dominated a low knoll with deep shadows around it. Lute would be up there with Marge. His own two rooms were up there, too, but now there was something else up there. An obstacle he would never be able to surmount. Luther knew the whole story. He would tell Marge. Everything was changed.

He turned and looked down the length of his town. No, not everything. Sageland was still the same. People and animals, noise and the new smells, clanging anvils, lazy dust and riders swinging in towards the liverybarn with wide looks at the prosperity of the place. He belonged down there anyway. Moving again, his chin thrust forward as though to meet life head-on, he went back down as far as the hotel, and there he ordered that two rooms be permanently set aside for him. There was no argument in spite of the fact that the place was even then doubling up its transient guests. He owned the building.

Then he walked south where the livestock corrals were, lit a cigar and strolled among the trading groups. It didn't matter that he no longer traded. Just being among the bustle, the arguments, the lies and solemn promises, the deceits and humours, always pleased him. Here was one aspect of the old days he always got a thrill out of. Horse trading.

Now he strolled among the little clutches of men, listening to their talk, seeing their gestures, their exaggerated expressions of near-saintliness, their pocketknives and their whittling sticks. It was a part of the real west destined to outlive all the rest. He sensed it then as he had before, and he enjoyed it. It drew his mind away from other things.

But it took a long time for his inner spirits to rise again, and when they did, finally, he was established in his new rooms at the hotel. Luther came to see him there, more sombre than ever. Forge set out the traditional Irish whiskey and cigars. For once Lute ignored both as he lowered himself to a chair and watched Forge pour a staggering drink and down it.

"Why'd you move out of the house, Forge?"

The brittle blue eyes fixed themselves reprovingly on Lute. "That's a damn fool question," he said. "You know why, and I reckon Marge does, too, by now."

Luther studied his brother thoughtfully. "I reckon we'd better talk a little," he said mildly.

Forge broke in swiftly, ardently. "Not about her, Lute. I told you that before."

"Well, Forge, she'll be behind it all the way, I'm afraid."

"What do you mean?"

Luther changed his mind, poured out a stiff drink and downed it neat. His eyes watered and his face reddened. "I guess the best way's just to start right off, isn't it?"

"Go ahead."

"Forge — the first time we worked together it wasn't bad. The second time you were a little different. You've been changing more every day, since then." The gentle blue eyes were cloudy. "Oh — I guessed what it was, all right, but men get over those things. I just never guessed how bad it was. The little girl, I mean."

"That's a damned lie, Lute."

Luther shook his head. "I'm not so sure." He saw the anger rising in his brother's face. "Now, wait a minute, Forge. Just calm down and wait a minute. I didn't come up here to fight with you. What you've done is your business; right or wrong isn't what I'm here about."

"Then — whatever it is — get it off your chest, will you?"

Luther regarded Forge stonily. He ducked his head once, quickly, like a man jumping into icy water. "All right. It amounts to this. I don't want to sell out here like we've done before. This is good country. The land's rich and the cattle are doing good. There's a fortune here."

"In other words, Lute, you're satisfied. You never were an easy man to move. Now you want to drop out and stay up there in that barn of a house and live out your life there. Is that it?"

"That's it," Luther said. "We've talked it over."

"Sure you have," Forge said. "You and your wife." The bitterness was growing in him steadily, like the whiskey fumes that were filling his mind. "Lute — you always were pretty easy to satisfy. A damned brushranch, some scrawny old cows, a good spring and a shack."

"I had happiness, too," Luther said softly, his eyes beginning to smoulder. "You never had that, I reckon, or you'd know that's worth more than all this money, Forge."

"Happiness!" Forge stood up, leaning forward from the waist with one fist knuckle-down on the table-top.

"Money *is* happiness. A man's happiness. A woman — maybe that's different, but they want their happiness through money, Lute. What it'll buy. A big house and wood floors, clothes and what-not. What money'll get them, that's all they care about. That's how they measure happiness."

"You're a fool," Luther said resonantly, with pity ringing in his voice. "You've driven yourself hard. Too hard, Forge. Even Marge says that. You've got the money now. More'n either of us ever knew there was in the world. We're rich men and we've got a town and one of the biggest, best ranches in the country, and you're so blind you can't see that this is as far as a man can go.

"There's no sense to selling all of this and doing it over again. Not any more, Forge. We've got everything we worked for and wanted — and a lot more. That's why I want to settle down now." Luther ran his damp palms together. "If you want to keep on developing things — running from something — losing yourself in work — go ahead, but from here on, you're on your own."

Forge regarded his older brother stonily. "You're quitting," he said. "Up and quitting."

Luther stood up. "Quitting? Hell's bells, Forge, what else do we need that we haven't got or haven't the money to buy? Nothing. We've both earned peace and a long rest. That's what I want. Not more money."

Forge let his glance drop away. He sat down again, slowly. He played a dirge with his fingertips on the edge of the table. "How about what we own jointly?"

Luther remained standing. He shrugged as though this part of the conversation was especially distasteful to him. "Split it up any way you want to. Have the papers made out and put on my desk. I'll be down in a week or so to sign 'em."

Forge looked up. "Week or so? You two going away again?"

"Any objections? That's what we enjoy. That's where we get our happiness, being together and travelling a little." The warm blue eyes gazed downwards. "We haven't any kids, you know, so there's no happiness for us in that direction."

Forge steadied his glance coldly. There had been no irony in the words. He searched his brother's face. All he saw there, however, was melancholy. He drummed faster on the table and looked out of a window. "Well — how do you want the pardnership split up?"

"I don't care."

"You want the main ranch, I know that. All right — I'll deed over my share to you. I'll take Sageland. Is that agreeable?"

"Suits me fine." Luther took up his hat and fingered its brim. "The deals that're in process now — how'll we handle them?"

Forge arose again. The restlessness was eating at him. "Split 'em down the middle, I reckon. Half to you, half to me. There won't be many anyway, as far as I know. A few town lots and one or two pieces of acreage."

"I endorsed two new ones recently. Three west-side lots to that church outfit, and four hundred acres to a man named Knowlton."

It was like being kicked in the stomach by a mule. Forge almost sagged from it. He looked into his brother's face with a hushed, stilled expression of pain and anger both. "Asa Knowlton?" he asked softly.

"Yes. Do you know him?"

"I told that scoundrel we wouldn't sell him any land around here under any circumstances." The vehemence of it startled Luther. His eyes opened wider and some of the previous discomfort vanished from them.

"Why? He seemed like a respectable feller to me. Besides, he paid all cash."

Forge almost groaned. "Does he have the deed yet?"

"Yes. I sent it down to him just before I came up here this morning. Forge, what's wrong? What's the matter with him?"

But Forge didn't answer. He lit a cigar and turned so that his face was hidden. Luther stood there with his doubt and anxiety both plaguing him. Forge's idiosyncrasies, his quick rages and his brusqueness had advanced to where it was difficult to understand him any more. That, even more than what Luther had been sickened by at the office when CarrieLee was there, had determined him to break with his younger brother.

Ever since that day, years back, when Forge had come leading his Pothook horse through the grey dawn with a ravaging illness in his heart, he had been changing. With each phase of their success he had changed still more. Where Luther stood now, he could see a dark and malignant destiny swooping low for his brother and it frightened him. Forge wouldn't be made to see, either. It was hopeless. Luther wanted to get clear of it all and yet he felt an overwhelming, if tongue-tied, pity for Forge, too.

Now this Knowlton. What possible reason could Forge have for his savage, unreasoning hatred of the man? None that Luther could see. Knowlton had told him he had been in Sageland only a few days; had never been west before. It didn't make sense — any of it — but it *did* make pain and unhappiness for the placid, gentle nature of Luther and he wanted an end to that once and for all. He watched Forge's broad back and picked up his hat again, turned it with his fingers while a fist squeezed his heart.

"Well — I reckon I'll go." Forge didn't move. Luther tried again. "Anything you want me to do back east? We'll be in Cincinnati and Chicago and maybe New York again."

"No."

Luther waited a moment longer. Forge didn't move; he was obscured by the cigar smoke. Luther went to the door and called back softly, "Adios, Forge," then he went out and the silence hung like a pall, behind him in Forge's room.

Knowlton — the underhanded scoundrel — had gone back when Forge wasn't in, met Lute, and bought the land anyway. The whiskey in him was dark behind his scowl. She'd done it. He could see through it if his fool brother couldn't. Because she was determined to haunt Forge Windsor. And she was going to marry that big ox of a Knowlton, too.

He swung back towards the table with a ragged curse. That's all marriage meant to her. Love? She had none in her scheming heart. He had thrown her out and she had bounced right back into this Knowlton's arms. Love! He laughed with a bitter harshness that only he heard.

Well; she'd worked it cleverly enough and now she'd be in Sageland. He'd sell out one day, of course, but in the meantime he'd have to see her. She'd see to that. What was it she'd said? Something about neither she nor God would let him forget . . .

He took refuge like he always did, in work. The days spun out into a soft, warm haze that was Indian summer. Leaves grew scarlet and yellow and finally, dying-silver. Winds came in the evening to soothe the sagebrush sea that was being pushed back under the land-clearing crews of the Windsors and the floating fragrance of burnt ashes flavoured the tangy fall air. Forge noticed none of it.

He had the communal properties split right down the middle and, where that was impossible, with an abandoned scorn he flung what was left to Luther. The reckoning surprised him. Liquidated, his assets were enormous. He had been too busy amassing to count; now he saw it all in dollars and cents and properties and his personal fortune was staggering. So was Luther's. More than enough to keep them both in luxury for their remaining lives, and yet Forge was still in his early thirties. Luther was older.

Sageland had served them well. It was still serving them profitably. There was every reason to believe it was going to do even better in the future. He pondered over that. There would be years and years of wealth to be accrued yet. If he sold out his interests the new owners would capitalise tremendously on what he had created and he would have to find another place and do it all over again. Lute was a little right, at that, after all.

Winter came with its howling blasts from the north. Sageland drew into itself and a lot of the activity ceased. Forge took a top-buggy and went out over the emigrant trail farther west. With his uncanny foresight he bought more land. It adjoined what was the farthermost reaches of Sageland's environs. The price was higher than he had expected it to be, but in an ironic way that amused him. He was the cause of the increased valuation, himself. By creating his town, he had also boosted land values around it.

After that he worked through the early winter nights plotting out into blocks and lots and roadways his new acquisitions, always bearing in mind the route of the emigrant trail westward.

By spring it was all green again with a warming sun to make it rich and enticing. Then he threw it open for sale and business grew to be more than he and two clerks could handle. Once, later in the summer, Luther rode down from his hilltop and walked through the thronged, buzzing land office. His face was fuller, more placid and gentle-looking than ever. Forge saw him and waved him into the office.

Luther accepted the tumbler of whiskey and smiled a little. Forge was amazed to see a showing of grey over his brother's temples. It made him abruptly aware of something he hadn't considered lately; the passing of time.

"How was the trip?"

"Pretty good," Luther said with a thoughtful glance into the glass he held. "You ought to take one."

"Why?" The defensive antagonism was rising in Forge.

"It gives you another view of this migrating urge that's all over the country, Forge. You wouldn't believe it. Why, as far away as Canada, people are talking about the west."

Forge nodded with a hard smile. "That's good. We can handle a lot more than we can get through here."

Luther drank and set the glass down. "It's a little bewildering sometimes. Where are they all going? The land'll be overflowing one of these days."

"Let'er overflow," Forge said, half in humour, half in earnest. "As long as they want the west, I'll sell it to them."

After he said it the echo came back and made him conscious of saying "I," not "we."

"There's trouble coming, too," Luther said gravely, either ignoring or not heeding Forge's remark. "Slavery's a real threat to the Union. Out here we don't hear much, but back east it's damned serious."

Forge had heard a little. Rumours and re-told tales. He shrugged. "That'll only drive 'em out here faster. There'll be those that'll run from the prospect of going into an army or fighting a war."

Luther raised his glance. "That's one way of looking at it," he said.

"How else?" Forge shot right back. "We don't own niggers. We have no stake in it, have we?"

"Not," Luther said in the same slow tone, "if we aren't Americans — I reckon we haven't. It'll mean a break-up of the Union, Forge, not just the nigger question. The United States against the Slavery States."

Forge held his peace but his thoughts were frank enough. Let'em fight. This was the west. It had enough of its own fighting with the damned Indians. Anyway — just when he was buying more land and business was booming like it never had before — this had to come along. He lit a cigar and let his cold eyes rake over his brother.

"Lute; how long'll it take before the fighting starts? The shooting and credit restrictions, and all — or will it come to that?"

"To fighting, yes. I'm afraid it will. The way I sized up the question back east, Forge, is that both sides are getting ready to fight right now. Oh — it'll be a year or so maybe, like it was with the Mexican War, but you can see the signs all right."

"Can't you call it closer than that?" Forge asked.

Luther wagged his head and smiled crookedly. "I don't reckon anyone can. A year maybe; two years. Maybe even longer. There's talk it'll break out even sooner, but personally, I doubt that. You can't wage a war like you do a gunfight. It takes time to get ready. I reckon both sides know that. I'm sure the North does. Why?"

Forge answered gruffly. "Because I've got some pretty big blocks of land, Lute. If there's going to be a rush out of the east and south I want to know about it so's to get all I can from my land. Hell; I don't want to undersell myself."

"No," Luther said slowly. "No, you wouldn't want to do that, would you?" He left after that and Forge watched him all the way through the busy office to the street entrance — and there, standing against the counter talking to his chief clerk, he saw another man. Asa Knowlton.

The reaction within him was swift. Almost automatic. He caught a clerk's eyes and sent for the man who was talking to Knowlton. While he waited he paced his office with cigar smoke trailing in his wake like the gusts from an Indian signal-fire. The clerk entered and Forge faced him.

"Tom; what's that Knowlton feller want in here?"

"The adjoining section to him, Mister Windsor."

Forge's blue eyes were like thawing ice under a hot sun, wet and cold and bleak-looking. "He's got four hundred acres. Tom; I want you to block off all the land we own that surrounds his damned four hundred acres and show it on the books as my personal property and not for sale. Do you understand?"

"Yes, Sir," the clerk fidgetted. "Right now?"

"Right damned now!"

"Well — Mister Windsor — he's going to think it's odd. We've been going over it on the maps."

The vein in Forge's neck began to swell. "He can think whatever he wants to, Tom. If I had my way he wouldn't even have that four hundred. Now go back there and block out that surrounding land. Every section of it, then have it made over into a personal deed to me, in my own name."

"Yes, Sir."

After the clerk had left, Forge walked heavily across the room to his desk. There was a hard core of ruthless triumph in him. He sat down at the desk and thumbed through the deeds left there for his signature. A loud knock brought his head up.

"Come in!"

Asa Knowlton threw back the door and filled the opening. Forge was surprised. Their glances held in the long silence, then Knowlton came into the room farther and closed the door. He had a wicked expression on his face. "Why did you withdraw that land, Mister Windsor?" he asked softly.

Forge stood up slowly, his features settling into a granite look. "Why? Because I wanted to, Knowlton. Does that answer your damned impertinent question?"

Knowlton's face darkened and he walked over to the edge of Forge's desk before he shook his head and spoke. "No, it doesn't. For some reason I'm at a loss to understand, you've deliberately set yourself up as a personal enemy to me. I have no reason to believe I've ever harmed you, but if I have and you'll be man enough to tell me how — I'll correct the situation here and now."

"There is only one way you can correct the situation," Forge said harshly, "and that is to sell me back the land you bought through my brother, and get to hell out of this country!"

"Why?" Knowlton asked, anger making his face pale.

"Because that's the way I want it."

Knowlton relaxed a little. Along with the rancour in his gaze was scorn as well. "You're not man enough to tell me what's caused this dislike, are you?"

Forge held his temper with a great effort. His hands were trembling and he knew it. He put them both on his desk and leaned on them, looking up at the larger, older man. "I'm under no obligation to tell you a damned thing, Knowlton, now or ever, nor will I, unless it suits me to do so."

Knowlton's big hands drew slowly into massive fists at his side. "I thought you'd be like that," he said slowly. "You're the kind to wear success like it was a club."

Forge hit him. It was a wild, raging blow that staggered Knowlton even though the desk was between them. With an inarticulate curse Forge followed it up. But Knowlton was hard. Harder than Forge was. He was a stolid man in many ways. Unimaginative, with few illusions. Even when he had married CarrieLee it had been with the knowledge that she respected him but didn't love him. He had expected nothing more than that and was satisfied with it. Now his frugality of spirit manifested itself. He neither smoked nor drank. He worked hard with his muscles. He was more than a match for Forge, who was fighting like a wild animal, spending his strength like a madman.

Knowlton took his stance and let Forge bring the fight to him. Forge did. He was no novice at rough-and-tumble either. He feinted the larger man without success, then he fired a vicious, killing blow that Knowlton rolled with and got back a battering-ram punch that knocked him down. Rolling swiftly, Forge got up with a bounce, but his lungs were bursting from the effort and he was a little dazed. He walked into the next blow head-on. It was so well aimed that the world came down around his head with a lot of pain in it, and he went down again. That time he stayed down.

Knowlton stared at Forge and rubbed his bleeding knuckles. He stood for a long time in reflection, then he stepped over the unconscious form and stalked out of the office, closing the door behind him.

When he was fully recovered, Forge was grateful for one thing. Knowlton had had the decency to close the door, and so far as Forge could learn, he never mentioned the fight to anyone.

That might have tempered Forge's animosity under any other circumstances, but in this case it didn't. He carried the memory of his defeat through another winter and on into the following summer, but it gradually faded from his mind with the press of business for, as Luther had predicted, a new wave of emigration was rolling westward.

Politics were in the air like Forge had never seen them before. One evening in late '59, he had the liveryman harness up his driving-team to the sombre black buggy he owned, and he drove all the way up to Luther's place on the hill. Marge, with poorly disguised surprise, welcomed him. She left him with his brother in the spacious, pleasant parlour and Luther poured the whiskey.

90

"Lute, you were right. It may even have happened by now, for all we know."

"The war?" Luther said. "It may have." He looked up swiftly at Forge. "How's business?"

"Better than ever." Forge sat back with his whiskey. The room inspired a peacefulness in him that felt strange. He crossed his legs. "I've been wondering, Lute. Do you reckon it'll touch us, out here?"

Luther shrugged. "Hard to say, Forge. Maybe not too much. We'll probably get a lot of people we wouldn't get otherwise. Money'll be cheaper."

"But cattle and horses'll be better than ever, Lute."

"I reckon. Hardware too. It's a poor way to make a profit, but there it is."

Forge snorted. "There's no such thing as a poor way to make a profit."

"No?" Luther said softly. "I don't want money made from men's blood and ideals."

They fell into an awkward silence after that, which was, basically, the underlying difference that was so strong between them. It was Luther who finally broke it.

"Have you heard the government's pulling out its frontier garrisons?"

"Well — I've heard that, but people get panicky and magnify things. The government wouldn't do that. That's not commonsense, Lute. If they did, the damned Indians'd be down around our necks in a matter of days. No — we're as much a part of the nation as the east or south. They won't do that."

Luther frowned at Forge. "They already have, over at old Fort Pike on the Colorado line."

"Not all the soldiers," Forge said stubbornly. "Hell, Lute — that's absurd. They may cut down the garrisons but you and I both know they'll always have to leave some here. And Pike, Lute — that's athwart the old Comanche Trail."

But Luther was adamant. "Forge, Marge and I came home this summer through Pike. It was just about deserted. There were a few cowmen still hanging around up there and no soldiers at all.

Forge looked long at his brother. "You mean they took them *all?*"

"Every one. The cowmen told me they were going to come down this way where there's protection for their livestock."

Forge was shaken. With the Colorados left unguarded, the whole sweep of the far reaches of Indiandom were at liberty to pour down across the prairies of Kansas. It was something Forge had trouble grasping. There had been no appreciable Indian trouble around the Sageland country in almost ten years. This was like rolling back the decades, inviting disaster for everything the settlers had laboured for.

The more he thought of it the deeper grew his depression. He set the untouched glass on a table and leaned forward on the edge of his chair. This was an altogether unexpected twist to a theme he was coming to accept. Civil war would come, the entire frontier knew that by now, but this other — this red peril from the northwest — was enough to stun him.

"The damned government," he said finally. "The damned blind government. What about us, out here, Lute?"

Luther lit a cigar. "I reckon the seat of the matter right now isn't the frontier, Forge," he said. "It's deeper and bigger than that. The nation's going to fight to preserve itself as a union of states and territories. I think that's more important than this country out here."

"*You* think so," Forge said hotly. "What the devil's got into you to say a thing like that, Lute? All we've worked for, built up . . ."

"We've got enough," Luther interrupted him. "We've got more'n enough."

"Damn it," Forge thundered. "You know these redskins. They'll run off the cattle, burn out the ranchers, scalp the kids. Why — it's madness to withdraw the troops."

"It'd be worse," Luther said, "if there *was* no United States."

The way he said it replaced the indignation in Forge with a strange, deep sensation of hollowness. He kept his glance on Luther but he said nothing. An incredible picture loomed in his mind. He hung there on the edge of his chair staring at his brother without seeing him. The dawning came slowly, painfully. He had been too engrossed with his fetish to more than listen to the talk of the town. The pulse of its life — the only thing he really listened to — had always been the ringing of the anvils, the lowing of cattle and the relentless grinding of huge wheels westward. He felt like a stranger in his own mind; a groping wanderer in a new world.

No United States? That would mean their fortunes too. He wasn't aware of his brother staring at him oddly, until Luther spoke.

"I reckon a man's got to think a little before he gets it all straight in his mind, doesn't he?"

Forge came back to the present slowly. He nodded. "If it's going to be like that, Lute, we've got to take steps to protect ourselves."

"Yes. I've been thinking that lately."

Forge's resentment lingered, even then. "Are they going to pull out *all* the troops?"

"I expect they'll leave a few, but not up here — no. This isn't really considered established country, Forge. Down along the border, over in Texas, places like that, they'll do what they can, but up here we're expendable. This is new country. Maybe they think they can come back here someday and reconquer it. I don't know; these are things a man thinks about." Luther didn't finish. He pushed the whiskey bottle towards Forge and leaned back in his chair.

Forge ignored the drink and the bottle. He was gazing out of the window at the limitless scope of country. "I reckon we'd better work things out," he said vaguely, his eyes pin-pointing the distance.

"What do you mean?"

"Defences, Lute. We've got a lot to protect. The town, your ranch, the cattle. We'd better organise the ranchers and townsmen. Work up some kind of a vigilante outfit so we'll be ready for them when they come."

Luther wasn't sure whether Forge meant the Windsor holdings exclusively or the entire community. He remained silent, thinking of the people far out who had built ranches and homes across the old Indian trails.

"I'll have a meeting called." Forge looked at his brother in the lengthening shadows. "You'll want to be a part of it, won't you?"

"Yes," Luther said dryly.

Forge stood up. "All right. Meet me at the office tomorrow afternoon. I'll have 'em herded into town by then."

Luther nodded wryly. "There's one thing I always admired about you, Forge. When you move, you move fast."

Forge's glance held his brother's eyes sardonically. "But that's about all you *do* like, isn't it?"

"I don't think this is the time to go into that," Luther said flatly.

Forge was almost to the door when Luther's wife stopped him. "Supper'll be ready pretty quick, Forge. Why don't you stay?"

He shook his head at her. "Thanks; no." He left the house on the hilltop and drove through the lingering twilight with the view of Sageland and the mighty sagebrush sea spread out around him like a gigantic painting.

The red and gold of the sunlight was splashed with a lavish stroke down over the country. There were bold saffrons farther westward where the bulwark mountains were. It was a scene that could move a man's soul. Forge's didn't move.

Luther stood beside his wife on the low porch and watched the lean man in the buggy move out against the sunset. "It's a funny thing," he said, "but, for a minute there, I thought Forge really saw the black future the way it is."

"How do you mean, Luther?"

"Well, not as a dollar sign. As a threat that'll make us all dependent on one another — sort of. It's hard to explain, Marge. Like something was going to make us all close together. Make us all equals. Like Forge felt that maybe, after all, money wasn't everything."

Marge's eyes clouded. She had no vast love for Forge Windsor. He was too cold, too calculating and withdrawn. He had been like that for so long it wasn't likely that he would ever change. She sighed and watched the buggy getting smaller.

"Do you really think the Indians'll come, Luther?"

"Come?" he said. "Of course they'll come. They'll be busy gleaning in their own country for a while, but when they get low on food and plunder, they'll come all right."

"It's frightening, isn't it?"

"I reckon," Luther said soberly. "It'll *be* frightening after you see what they leave behind them."

She felt for his arm and held it against her. "Wouldn't it be wiser for us to go away? Back to Chicago or — some place — until it's over."

"This is where we belong," Luther said. "If others don't run we won't either. If you believe in the destiny of a country, Marge, you don't just stay while the sledding is good." He smiled at her. "We owe this country a lot more than we can ever repay it — you know that. We'll stay."

"Yes, of course. You're right." She was moodily silent for a while. "Isn't the ranch pretty exposed, Luther?"

"We'll make out all right, honey. I'll have the riders drift the stock south onto the plains. We'll run the place like it's a fort. There'll be nighthawking to do just like on a drive. The boys'll be detailed to it. We haven't much to fear anyway, this close to town. It's those people way out I was wondering about."

"Like the Knowltons?"

"Yes."

"Luther — does he ever see her?"

Luther's glance drifted from his wife's face. "I don't think so. I never saw two people who worked harder at avoiding each other."

"She does," Marge said. "He doesn't. It isn't in him to avoid unpleasantness."

"She does a good job of it then. I'll bet he hasn't seen her in three years. That's not easy in a place the size of Sageland."

"It's the saddest thing I ever heard of, Luther."

He didn't respond. The night closed down softly. There was a taint of fall in the air. He thought: *A man can get as old as the Devil himself, and still be a boy. I never thought age was like that. I thought you got wisdom and tolerance with age, but you don't. You stay pretty much in the head as you always were. Maybe your joints stiffen and your hair greys and you slow down, but your hates seem to live forever.* A slight shiver swept through him. Marge felt it in the arm she was holding.

"Let's go in, Luther. Supper's ready."

CHAPTER
FIVE

Out of the North, a Scream . . .

Forge sent out riders from among his labour crews. They loped from ranch to ranch with wild rumours and the news of the mass-meeting. The land came quickly to life in the face of the new peril. People hitched up and saddled up, and just plain walked. Some brought their families, some didn't. Asa Knowlton brought only his oldest son, a gangling youth all angles and sharp corners with large grey eyes and surprising poise.

The meeting was held in Forge's Sageland Emporium building. There was a huge storeroom out back that had been hastily gotten ready. The smoke and warmth were thick and the plank seats loaded. Forge looked over at Luther, behind a desk similar to his own, and urged him to make the opening talk.

Luther did, with his warm, deep voice. He told them what had been done to the frontier by the government. How it had been stripped of soldiers and protection. He even justified the stripping with a prayer, almost, for the Union's preservation.

Even with Southerners among them — mostly Texans — Lute said that at present the greatest fight was the one back east, but the most imminent conflict to each of them here and now was the Indian danger. He finished speaking and sat down. The big storeroom was wrapped in deepest silence. Then a tall, red-faced man with a drover's whip looped carelessly over one shoulder stood up.

"Boys — I figger a man with a family's got no call to wait out here to get 'em all sculped. The safest thing to do is go back east until the danger's past."

"What's the difference," another man growled sourly, "whether ye get kilt here or back there in th' army?"

Forge had expected someone to disagree with what Luther had said. He lunged upwards out of his chair and held up his hand. "Wait a minute," he said. "I'm glad that's come up. It's best for us to thresh everything out here and now, then behind the barn." He was a lean, dominating figure. They all knew him. Many didn't like him, but they all knew who he was.

"I don't believe that fear should ever be a reason for a man not standing where he damned well wants to stand." He waited; no one challenged him. "This land is giving us our living. It's a good land; our cattle and horses thrive in it. Your kids do, too. No country on earth can give you more'n that. You've got freedom and the right to do what you want to do. Those things are worth fighting for. All the war-painted Indians in the west won't make me back up from where I stand."

A short, Irish-looking husk of a man got up with a determined thrust to his jaw. "An' how," he asked, "do

100

ye propose to stay alive ag'n these redskins? It's all fine an' good to talk — but a gun makes a hell o' a lot more noise than you do — 'specially an Injun gun."

Others joined in, agreeing with the Irishman. Forge was still standing. He gestured with his arm. The noise died away but not completely. Then Luther stood up and, to Forge's surprise, the store got as quiet as a tomb. He watched his brother's face and knew that Lute's character was better known — better liked — than his own. He sat down.

Luther spoke quietly. So quietly that the listeners had to keep their silence in order to hear him at all. "My brother and I have already talked this over, boys. We're staying. If you don't want to stay we don't blame you, but those who *are* going to stay, we want to organise into vigilante groups. If the Indians come they'll get a very warm welcome. As far as Indian guns are concerned — we've all faced them before, and when it comes to shooting — why — I reckon a settler's worth two redskins.

"Now then, those of you who plan to stay come on up here and sign your names to the town-rosters I've got. You'll be assigned different companies. We won't have anything like Army drill, but you'll be required to have a saddled horse ready at all times, as well as your guns, and we'll expect every man-jack of you to come running when you're called — *if* trouble comes. How does that sound to you?"

Forge watched them stamp their feet and stand up. Some shouted approval and others fell into heated arguments, but by far, the majority were swayed by

101

Luther's words. The west had a soul and this was it — the will of Westerners to fight anyone and any odds, to keep their own.

He got up and walked over where men were trickling in an increasing stream towards Luther. "Lute — give me some of those papers. I'll take half of them over there to sign up."

Luther handed over the sheets and raised his eyes briefly, then stiffened as Asa Knowlton came forward, towering over the others. He ignored Forge as completely as though he hadn't been anywhere near.

Looking over other heads at Luther, he said, "Mister Windsor; if there's any way I can help — I was an officer with General Taylor in Mexico."

Luther nodded and beckoned Knowlton forward. He didn't dare look at Forge although he sensed that his brother hadn't moved.

The press and clamour of men closed down over the brief enactment of antagonism and Forge was swept up by straining, boisterous volunteers.

The recruitment lasted a full two hours. Men who hadn't come to the mass-meeting heard of what had taken place and hurried forward to volunteer. With their lists, Luther and Forge went to the land office, sat down and totalled them.

"Quite a fighting force at that, Forge," the elder brother said with approval. "I didn't think there'd be that many that'd stay. Honestly and frankly, I figured about half of them would want to pull out with their families when they understood how things were."

"No," Forge said darkly, gruffly. "You're not giving them their due, Lute. They came out here to fight nature for a place in the sun. Nature means Indians, too."

Luther looked surprised. "By God," he said softly. "There's poetry in your soul after all, Forge. I never knew that."

Forge's irritation showed instantly. "Poetry? Poetry hell," he said sharply. "I deal in facts and nothing else. Now — how do you want to split up these men? I don't know the first thing about soldiering."

Luther leaned forward. "Me either. Those that show previous military experience I reckon ought to be the leaders. Don't you think so?"

Forge said, "Yes," then he saw Asa Knowlton's name and military record on the roster in front of him and his face darkened. "Here's Knowlton's name."

"What's it say behind it?" Luther asked it, knowing perfectly well what he had written there.

"With Taylor. Battles: Palo Alto, Resaca de la Palma, Matamoras — ."

"Well?"

Forge swung his head. The conflict in his eyes was unpleasant. "Damn him," he said bitterly.

"Forge, we need men like that. Don't let — ."

"I know it," Forge interrupted irritably. "I know it but that doesn't make me like him any better."

Luther said, "Well — fine. Now then, about the rest of it . . ."

His voice hurried on, a deep, pleasant drone that salved over the anger in his brother's face, then, when it

103

was all talked out, organised and tentatively agreed upon, he stood up, concentrating on Forge's face. "Send word to the men we think ought to be leaders and we'll have them all up to the ranch for a supper, Forge. That way we can get the details nailed down."

"Yeah, all right," Forge said, watching his brother leave and feeling the stirrings of rekindled kinship with Luther. It was a strange thing, in a way, for they had been almost strangers to one another for over a year now. Strange and warming, too.

But when it came time to go up to Lute's home on the knoll and sit in on the planning, Forge didn't go. He had no really valid reason for not going, he just didn't go. He couldn't have explained it to himself.

It wasn't because Asa Knowlton was there. They had come to look upon one another as portents of unpleasantness but under the current exigency they also realised the indispensable part each must play in the scheme of Sageland's protection and while they never spoke, they were at least in armed truce towards one another. It wasn't Knowlton, anyway. It was something inside him.

He walked through the warm, late summer night to the liverybarn. Sageland lay quiet and somnolent around him. The night was soft, benign, full of rich fragrance and the crisp tangyness of cooling sage. It was a smell he had always loved.

At the barn the nighthawk came out and wrinkled up his forehead at him. "Mister Windsor — you reckon all this talk about Injuns is likely?"

A little annoyed, Forge answered shortly. "People talk when they haven't anything better to do. There're Indians west of us — you know it and so does everyone else. Whether they get over here or not — I don't know."

"I heard today — from the stagedriver — there was some killings over by the Pike station."

"You'll probably hear a lot more than that before we know anything definite. There's danger, sure, but beyond that who can say? Get my rig, will you?"

He got his black buggy and drove out under the big, purple, inverted bowl of a sky with myriad lanterns winking overhead. The restlessness was in him. Why, he didn't know, just that it was. It wouldn't let him drive up the hill to Luther's and sit in the stuffy parlour, clouded with cigar smoke and ringing with voices, anyway, so he drove. Besides, he knew everything that was going to come out of the meeting.

He went without aim, following the ruts that meandered off over a country that still, largely, belonged to him, and out of the night loomed cabins. Some were strong, sturdy, frugal, built with the views of their owners in every line. Others were hastily thrown up and barely came under the description of homes at all. He could see little splashes of meagre light that fled from miserly window-slots and got lost in the great vault of darkness. He thought that within each soddie, each cabin, was a family.

It was an unusual sensation to him in a way, but he had never been completely unaware of the spirit of the emigrants either, and in his own hard, bitter way, he understood their dreams. He had shared them, once. It never occurred to him to envy them. The strength in him that success had bolstered kept softer emotions from intruding.

But the restlessness persisted as he drove. He lit a cigar and sat back against the quilted leather. Let the lines lie slack in his hands. Very grudgingly he let the barred doors of his mind open a little, in an effort to plumb the depths that led him to feel as he felt. Of course, the first wisp of thought to filter through his iron control was CarrieLee. He had known it would be; still, he maintained his inner grip so the thoughts didn't run wild and engulf him. It showed externally in the gauntness of his cheeks where the jaw muscles were locked on either side of clenched teeth, and in the erect, jutting thrust of the cigar.

She was out there somewhere with three children — one she had said was his. He didn't know where — had never looked up Knowlton's claim — had never wanted to know and didn't want to know now. And the child — he was curious about that. She had said it was a girl and that was improbable too, for in Forge's world were only men. Boys — his mind flicked up an image of Asa Knowlton's tall, ungainly son — at least boys grew to be men. Girls . . .

The red glow on the horizon caught his attention. A fire! There was always that fear. The people of Sageland, like the people of ten dozen other inland frontier towns, lived with that fear constantly before them every summer. The land grew dry and parched. The air was hot and dehydrated, sucked dry of

106

humidity. Anything could start a fire. Every precaution was observed from instinct, but the fear persisted, was very real, until after the first rains of fall.

He drove towards the glow wondering whose ranch it would be, and whether it was another stack of loose-hay, or perhaps a barn. The ruts weren't as deep now. From that, and the feel of his buggy bumping over them where the lumpy ground hadn't yet been ground flat under wagon wheels, he deduced that it was one of the places on the fringe of the settlement.

It didn't dawn on him that there was anything tragically wrong until he could smell the smoke, and by that time he was close enough to see the starkly etched outlines of the burning cabin.

A large cabin, one of those that showed the character of the man who had built it. A man whose thoughts didn't run only to grass and water for his cattle, but one of the few who laboured as hard to make his family comfortable as he did his animals.

By that time, Forge was close enough to see other people, too. Horsemen, wagoneers, even a few afoot, running towards the flames like apparitions in the darkness. He flicked his lines. The horse between the shafts moved faster. The buggy bounced and skittered over the uneven ground. He had to hunch forward on the seat and try to anticipate the jolts.

The flames had spread to a low, squatty barn. There was only the deep sound of them, roaring and crackling. Then he caught the sickening odour of burning flesh. It made his throat tighten up until breathing was difficult.

107

Closer still, he could see wraiths plunging across the background of terrible light, red at the outer limits and furious, twisting yellow in closer. The whole place was burning; house, barn, two smaller sheds and three ricks of hay that had been conical and built around hay-poles that still stood, aflame and grotesque in the brilliant, eyesearing light, like finger stumps through which charred bones protruded.

He laid on the whip and the buggy careened crazily until the heat made the horse veer away from it. Forge cursed, fighting the animal, then he gave it up with a leap that put him on the ground, hastily tied the horse to a handy juniper tree and ran forward afoot.

The heat was too intense. He lowered his head so his hat protected his face and kept on going. Someone grabbed his arm and pulled him violently back. He looked up into a vaguely familiar face. The features were greased with sweat and smudge. The eyes shone dryly.

"You can't get no closer."

"Where's the water brigade?" Forge shouted against the persistent roar of the flames.

"Ain't none. Can't get near the well. She's all agoin'. Can't stop her. Got to wait till she dies down a little."

"Where are the people?"

The dry-eyed man flung out an arm and looked past Forge. "Over yonder. Over where the womenfolk got blankets aroun' 'em."

"Was anyone trapped in there?"

"Naw. Folks say not. Couldn't none of us git to 'em to turn 'em loose — the animals I mean. That's what

108

the stink is. Horses and cattle that was in the sheds. Look at it burn."

Forge caught the man as he was shuffling off. "What started it?"

The man looked surprised. "You just got here, didn't you?" He raised one hand and crooked the fingers, beckoningly. "Come here," he said brusquely. "I'll show you."

They went where a silent, unmoving knot of men were staring at something inert that lay in the middle of their group, on the ground. The man jutted his chin downward with an angry, grim movement. His small, dry eyes, were hot-looking — hating. "There. That's what started it. One of 'em anyway."

Forge shoved roughly past the morbid ring of men and looked down. An Indian! The first thought he had at the sight of the corpse was what he whispered to himself, too softly for the others to hear.

"Already! Lord — they've started it already!"

He knelt, gripped the corpse by one tawny shoulder and flung it over, face up. There was a dark, almost black patch of dried blood on the savage's chest. Whoever had shot him had made it count. He probably never knew what hit him. It was directly between his bared breasts and through his breastbone.

"Right through his black heart," someone said with cruelly pleased tones. "The boy's a good shot."

Forge barely heard. He had come to know Indians passably well in his lifetime on the frontier. This one was a Comanche. A Comanche warrior — one of the most dreaded, if not *the* most dreaded — of all horse-Indians. The rank black hair had some Mexican coins worked into it. These caught the reflections of the raging flames and threw them back with an errie defiance into the night. There was a rifle near the body. A Springfield, Army-issue carbine of big bore and short range. A knife was sheathed and a bandoleer was lashed to the dead buck's waist. His body was naked from the waist up and marked with the symbols of his tribe and band, but his face was unpainted.

What held Forge's glance the longest, though, was a horsehair rope that was tied tightly around the Indian's ankle. It trailed off twenty feet or so, and there it was tied fast to another knife which was driven almost to the hilt in the flinty soil. He got up, following the thing with his eyes. A tall, almost cadaverously emaciated man next to him was looking at the same thing. He bobbed his head at the knife in the ground.

"Damndest thing the way they do that, ain't it?"

"What?" Forge asked quickly. "What's the meaning of it?" He turned and looked into the man's face. There was a sardonic hint of cold humour there. The blue eyes were thoughtful and baleful-looking.

"They've got those damned fools, like this one was, who want to show how much guts they've got. They ride in ahead of the others, tie that rope on 'em and stick the knife in the ground. It means they won't leave that spot until the fight's won or some other buck rides up and cuts them loose. Supposed to show that they're the bravest Injuns in the world."

110

Forge looked back down at the dead warrior. He felt a bitter surge of cruel pleasure. "This one made a mistake, didn't he?"

"Yeh. Most of 'em do," the tall, skinny man said laconically. "I've seen 'em do that stunt, by God, right in front of a charging troop of dragoons." The man's smile flickered self-consciously at Forge. "Fact is, one time I near cut the head off one — when I was in the army." The man spat an amber stream of tobacco at the ground.

Forge turned away from him. The group around the dead Comanche was growing. He saw a man who worked in the liverybarn and went over to him.

"Sam. Form up a bucket-brigade as soon as you can get near the well." He let it dribble off into silence for, in looking past the man, he could see that there wasn't going to be anything to save. Everything was burning; the fire was too hot. "Never mind that, Sam," he corrected himself. "Where are the survivors?"

"Over yonder, Mister Windsor. 'Feller's away at your brother's place at the meeting. The lady and kids're yonder where the other womenfolk're milling around."

"Sam — my buggy's down the lane. Fetch it up here and take them back to town in it. Have them put up in my rooms at the hotel. Roust up the hotel's cook to feed them. If they need the doctor, hunt him up too."

"Yes sir, but how'll you get back to town?"

Forge shook his head irritably. "I'll get back. I'll borrow a horse somewhere."

"Oh," the hostler said suddenly. "You can have mine. He's a blaze-faced sorrel with a Mex saddle. I tied him over in the willows ahind the house and back a little."

"Good," Forge said. "I'll go get the people. Sam — you bring my buggy up closer here."

He turned swiftly and edged his way through the white, glistening faces that had motionless, helpless bodies attached. He saw the forlorn hopelessness in every face. There was nothing anyone could do. Nothing. That was the worst of a thing like this. Standing around watching a man's sweat and pain and labour, his hopes and plans, all go up in smoke.

The women who had come with their menfolk to help, after the custom of the country, were clustered. There were hastily made sandwiches, canteens with coffee and tea, blankets that made the survivors look like Indians themselves. Dejected, dull-eyed Indians.

He mumbled and twisted his way through the throng of people and saw the boy first. He was fully as tall as Forge was, but thin. There was bewildered anguish in his face and his white hands were plucking unconsciously, spasmodically, at a quilt someone had thrown around his shoulders.

Forge moved into the boy's vision, blocked it, and watched the stunned, apathetic eyes lift to his face. He reached out and took the boy by the arm, pulled him away from the crowd. Led him away from the others, mindful of his dutiful but sluggish gait, motioned for the lad to sit on a jumble of saddlery someone had managed to haul to safety before the fire became unbearable, and squatted in front of him. He studied

112

the grey, slack face. There was something remotely familiar about it which Forge ignored. He saw dozens of people everyday and remembered only those he wished to remember.

"Tell me about it," he said. "Which way did they come, how long they were here — all of it."

The youth's eyes held their deep-lying shock and bewilderment when he began to speak. "Ma saw them first. That was after the horses nickered in the barn and we figured dad was coming home. I opened the door to hold a lantern for him and one of them let out a scream." The boy held back part of a shudder. "I — we — barred the door and Ma got the guns. Maria commenced crying and — ." He shook his head suddenly. There was a liquid shininess to his eyes that reflected the wild firelight. Forge reached over and put a hand on his shoulder. Shook him a little, gently.

"Not now. You can do that later. Right now talk it out. There's nothing better for you. Spit it out, boy."

"We shot at them. One came up real close ahead of the others. He was afoot. He was bent over a lot of the time like he was doing something to his foot. I waited. He wasn't a hundred feet in front of my loop-hole. When he got up I shot him. He's — over there."

"I know," Forge said. "I saw him." He looked at the thin face, the enormous eyes with their unseeing, inward expression, and the white lips drawn back tightly. Pity trickled through him. "I've got a hundred dollars and the best damned — darned — horse in Sageland for a feller who can shoot like that.

113

"Now then — how many did it look like there were of them?"

"Many? I don't know. 'Looked like a million."

"Twenty maybe? Fifty?"

"Maybe twenty. I couldn't tell. They rode around a lot and some ran into the barn and the cow-shed and started fires in there. Maria was screaming and running around in the house. I couldn't — ."

"Which way did they go when they left?"

The boy raised his arm and pointed westward with it. "That way," he said. "They didn't ride off until everything was on fire. They waited, but we didn't come out. Ma wouldn't let us; only Maria kept — ."

"Yeah, I know. She was crying and scared. Is she your sister?"

"Yes — only she's a lot younger'n us boys. She's just a little kid. She's not really our — ."

"Who was hurt, in the house?"

"None of us got hurt. They must've been scared off. Ma said if they hadn't been scared off we'd of had to come out of the cabin while they were still around, and if we'd had to do that, she said — with the light behind us — ."

"Sure," Forge said soothingly, "I understand. How soon was it after they started the fires that folks began riding in?"

"Darned soon," the boy said, rousing a little. "Gee — it seemed like the Morleys were here'n less than half an hour."

"Are they your closest neighbours?"

114

"Yes. Ma said the Indians must've heard 'em coming."

Forge got up and flexed his legs. The heat on his back seemed to be diminishing but it was still dreadfully hot. He looked around at it and saw that the barn, sheds, even the big log house, had all collapsed and were lying in prostrate ruin with flames flashing upwards thirty feet and more, straight into the still, night air. He turned back to the boy, who had also arisen and was standing there looking dully at what had been his home. He was plucking with one white hand at Forge's coatsleeve.

"Will you go after her, Mister?"

Forge was puzzled. "After who?"

"After Maria. That's what I tried to tell you. They got her."

A sinking sensation filled Forge. "I'm sorry," he said. "I didn't understand what you were trying to say. Maria — that's your little sister; you mean they got *her*?"

"Yes. She got the bedroom window open and got outside. She was always scared of fire. She was screaming and runnin' around in the house and we couldn't watch her an' she got out — outside."

"How old is she?"

"Five or six, I reckon. Maybe seven. I don't know for sure."

There was the smallest of consolations in that, Forge knew. No Comanches — no Plains Indians, in fact — ordinarily killed captive children, unless they were pursued or burdened by their prisoners. "I'll do what I

115

can," he said shortly. "Now — you see that black buggy the man just drove up, over there?"

"Yes."

"Go get in it. The driver's going to take you back to town for the night."

"But, my mother's here," the boy protested.

"I know," Forge said. "I'll fetch her. You just head for the buggy."

The boy turned without another word and ambled towards Forge's rig. He was more slumped now than he had been before, as though talking about what had happened had burdened him with a staggering weight, some way.

Forge turned back and wound his way through the people. There were two things to do. Get the settlers cared for, then go after the little girl. He allowed himself no reflections on either. As Luther said, when he decided to move, he moved.

Men were beginning to edge in closer to the well-box. They had buckets and averted faces. It was a gesture only. An automatic, frontier instinct. There was nothing left that dousing the flames could salvage.

He got past the clutch of grey-faced women. Over near where the woman with the blanket around her stood. There was a younger boy by her side. He could see the way she was clinging to his hand. He took her by the elbow and spoke with his face towards the people who blocked their passage towards the buggy.

"Come along, ma'm. There's a buggy over here that's going to take you into town to the hotel. I'll have your husband sent for."

He was impatient with the people who barely moved and frowned his way through them with slow progress. Beyond them, out in the clear and with the fire behind them and a coolness in their faces, he could hear the shouts of men and the angry hissing that arose from the red-hot places where the water struck. He turned his head and gazed at her with a mechanical and reassuring smile. The buggy was just ahead, his man was waiting and the other boy was already . . .

"CarrieLee!"

Her grey eyes had been watching his face for moments before he turned. The enormity of their meeting, the devastation they were pilgrimaging through, shocked him motionless. He stopped as though struck, let go of her arm and felt the quick pounding of blood into his face.

"CarrieLee."

"Forge — they got her. They took Maria. I — we — looked for her. There was only this." She held up a little ragged piece of plaid cloth. "It's part of her dress."

"Your daughter?" he said dumbly, still stunned at their meeting.

She held his glance easily because he hadn't tried to look away from her yet. Then she shook her head at him, bent and touched the boy's face at her side and looked over at the buggy. "Honey; go climb into the buggy. Willie's already over there — see?" The lad regarded the vehicle dubiously, saw his brother finally and moved away. CarrieLee straightened up with a depth of agony in her eyes. "No, Forge," she said firmly,

117

with the hissing, blood-coloured wreckage behind her. "Not just my daughter. Your daughter as well."

Words came boiling slowly but savagely to his lips, but he clamped down hard, and held them back. Regardless — it was a little girl. A very small, terrified little girl out there in the night with fierce, dark faces around her. It didn't matter that her mother lied; it was anyone's little girl.

He was framing a cold answer when CarrieLee moved still closer, never taking her eyes off him, looking up at him with the red-yellow glow of the dwindling firelight shining fitfully across one side of her face.

"Don't let them kill her, Forge. She's all I have to remind me of better days — better things. Please — don't let them hurt her."

The stiffness remained, but the contempt in him dissolved. Like her little girl — it didn't matter who she was or what she was — what was before him was a mother pleading desperately for her daughter. He hadn't felt the same shaken pathos since old Tim Dolan had died.

He turned on his heel towards the buggy and beckoned to the driver. There was that knife-edged, thin white strip, above his upper lip. The horse came slowly, reluctantly, tossing its head in the face of the increased heat. She had time for just a little more.

"Forge — you don't have to believe me. I don't really care whether you do or not. I don't expect that any more, but don't let them take her away from me."

"Get in," he said shortly, when the buggy was close enough. He didn't offer her his hand but went around

118

to the driver's side of the vehicle without another glance at her. "Sam. As soon's you get back ride hard for my brother's house. Tell him and Asa Knowlton to round up as many men as they can and follow my trail. Tell them I'm going to take as many men as I can from here, and start after the Indians now. Tell them — there's a little girl been stolen. Mrs. Knowlton's daughter. Tell them to be careful, the Indians'll kill her if they know a big party's behind 'em." He started to turn away, remembered something and turned back again just as the buggy was starting to move. "Sam? Is there a carbine on your saddle?"

"Yes, Mister Windsor, an' she's a good 'urn too. 'You got plenty shells?" Sam's hands were moving as he spoke. He threw something towards Forge. "There's extras, Mister Windsor — I hope to God you get to use 'em. I'll tell the others."

Forge moved swiftly towards the cursing line of fire-fighters. There was nothing they could do that hadn't already been done. He saw that while he walked towards them. There was nothing left of the Knowlton ranch but the land. The house area was a place of charred ruin, blackness, sour smells and heartbreak. It fed his ire to see the wanton ruin. He was the old Forge Windsor again, implacable, hard-driving, brusque and dominating.

A tall, sweaty man loomed up before him. He recognised the face as the man who had stood beside him talking about the dead warrior. He strode closer, speaking as he moved. "You there. What's your name?"

119

The bony face came around slowly, the eyebrows climbed a little at the harshness of the question. For a moment the man regarded Forge with mild hostility, then he said, "Waite Hefner — why?"

Forge fired words at him. "Waite — round up every man you can find that has a horse here, a carbine, and a pistol."

Understanding replaced the coolness. Hefner said, "Sure. Be proud to. You're Mister Windsor — aren't you?"

"Yes. Send everyone you find over where that clump of willows is behind the — where the house used to be. Bring along your own horse, too. We'll ride."

He watched the lean man move among the groups of men, then turned and went over where the hostler had said he'd left his saddle horse. The noise of the fire was dying and in its place was the noise of voices.

Forge was examining the blaze-faced sorrel with the Mexican saddle when mounted men began to ride up out of the splotchy night. Some men came afoot, on the off-chance there might be an extra horse they could borrow. Every face told the same story. They were ready. Forge led the blocky sorrel horse by the split-reins. He threw the shell-belt the horse's owner had tossed at him from the buggy across the saddlehorn, and watched the men dismount and converge on him. The last to come was a skeleton a-horseback. That was Waite Hefner.

Until that moment Forge only recalled two things about the man. One was his knowledge of Indians, the other thing was what Hefner had said about having been a soldier. That was good. Now, though, there was something else he noticed as the tall man rode up. Texan. It was written all over Hefner. In the split-ear bridle, the Santa Cruz bit, the three-quarter-double rigged saddle with the flat, larger-than-normal horn. In the viciously small-roweled spurs he wore, and in his general appearance. Texan.

Forge shrugged. Yankee — Texan. Right now they were frontiersmen and a little girl had been carried away by the Comanches.

"Everyone got a carbine and a pistol and a horse?"

Not all of them had carbines but all of them had pistols. Those without horses were silent, waiting, hoping.

"Well — have you all got plenty of pistol ammunition then?" They had. "Good. Now listen to me. We're going after those Comanches." He counted them as he talked. Nine. Not very many but there was nothing he could do about that, either.

"We'll spread out but keep in sight of one another. We'll ride due west. That's the direction they're supposed to have taken. Watch for signs. It'll be hard to see and maybe we won't cut any at all before sunup, but we'll keep going anyway. We've got to make time, boys. They've got the little girl from here."

"What little girl?" someone called out sharply.

"There was a little girl in the house. She jumped out of a window. Her mother found a piece of her dress. They've got her, sure."

Someone swore in a stifled voice. It was Waite Hefner. Forge shot a hard glance to silence him. The Texan didn't silence but he changed over into coherence. "Is her daddy among us?"

"No," Forge said. "What's that got to do with it?"

"This," Hefner said shortly. "They kill captives if they're pushed. Brain 'em an' leave 'em lyin' to slow down pursuit. It'd be better if her daddy was along. It's his responsibility."

"It's every man here's responsibility," Forge said loudly, coldly. "We've got to try and get her back and not dilly-dally around until her father can get here from Sageland. Every hour counts. We'll trail them but not get too close. In the first place we don't want to get the child hurt, in the second place I think we're damned well out-numbered."

"They'll head up into the Rockies," Hefner said. "From up there they'll be able to see us trailin'."

"There's no other way," Forge shot back exasperatedly. "I'm not going to stand here and argue about it, either. Either we go after her and risk her being killed, or we let her go and they'll kill her anyway."

He waited. Hefner lapsed into silence. None of the other men had an opinion to express one way or the other. Forge swung up, shot a dark glance back at the ruin, beyond which he could make out dark silhouettes that were people, moving aimlessly. The riders edged up a little closer. He turned and looked them over again. They weren't many but every one of them looked capable.

122

"Don't get out of sight of your nearest neighbour. Watch for their tracks and the first one who runs across them let out a yell." He stopped talking, tightened his grip on the reins and was about to move when a ruddy-faced man, who was hatless and with a great mop of dirty-looking blond hair, pointed at the shell-belt encircling the huge Mexican horn of Forge's saddle.

"If you don't need all the pistol shells in that 'ere belt, Mister Windsor, I'd sure admire to have a few."

Forge leaned over and flung the belt to the man. "Give me back the carbine bullets," he said, wheeled and led off. The tall Texan was beside him. He turned and looked into the sunburnt face.

"Were you ever at Fort Pike?"

"No, not at Pike. I was at Conejos Camp in the San Juans up above the New Mexican line. Why?"

"We need someone who knows that country westward towards the mountains. I don't, and I don't expect any of the others do. If we have to trail them very far, we'll need someone to guide us."

"Well," Hefner said slowly, "I reckon I can do that all right. At least I know the general fall of the country, if not the trails and such-like."

Forge nodded. "That's plenty good," he said. "You ride along with me."

"Did you send back for help?" Hefner asked. "Nine white men aren't much good against more'n nine Comanches."

Forge eyed the taller, thin man wonderingly. "You have a high opinion of Indians," he said.

"Not Indians, no; but of Comanches — yes. I've fought 'em before. They're worse'n Apaches by a damned sight. I know. Did you?"

"Yes. I told the man who drove my buggy back to town what we were going to do and for the town to make up a posse and follow after us."

Hefner seemed vastly relieved. He twisted backward in the saddle and looked at the lumpy shadows that were coming along behind them, grunted and fell back into silence.

They rode westward through the darkness with a wisp of cold air hitting them on the north side. Forge sniffed at it; dawn wasn't far off. He was surprised. The entire night couldn't be spent — could it? He brought out his watch and flicked back the cover to peer at the face. Five o'clock straight up. Unbelievable; it seemed only an hour or so before that he'd ridden out from Sageland with his consuming restlessness, and saw the flames on the horizon.

The little band fanned out when they got clear of the heavy brush. The air was bracing but the night was like ink. Forge tried to see the ground beneath the sorrel's quick-moving hooves and couldn't. Waiting for enough dawn light to see by was aggravating, but he felt they were going in the proper direction, if for no other reason than because it was the easiest, most logical route for horsemen to travel through the sagebrush sea.

Hefner spoke suddenly, catching Forge's wandering attention. "They'll more'n likely make a bee-line for some camp or other."

124

"Why do you say that?"

"Well — they don't like to have prisoners along with a war-party. Especially kids or women. I reckon a woman-child'd be just about the worst thing they could keep along, the way they look at things. Bad luck."

"But you don't think they'd kill her — do you?"

Hefner threw him a long, saturnine look, before he answered. "Sure I do. I think they may've killed her already, if you want to know what *I* think — but I don't think we can just drop out either, so we'd best keep right on going until we find out, one way or the other."

"They don't kill captives, I've been told."

Hefner began to make a cigarette, his horse slogged along with the reins flopping. "Who can say what they'll do?" he said. "Boys — no — they don't kill them unless the kids give 'em a reason. They can make warriors out of boys. Girls — that's different. White girls don't hold up so well, when they're worked by Indians. They get sick and die. Indians — Comanches 'specially — don't like to be bothered with 'em. If it's a real hells-fire warrior band — I don't think they'll keep her very long." He lit his cigarette and exhaled without looking at Forge.

CHAPTER
SIX

Drinkers of the Wind . . .

The nine men jogged through the lightening sky and the grey daybreak with faces greasy with sweat and dirt. Their whisker stubble gathered dust and made gaunt shadows; made them thoroughly disreputable-looking.

With the first soft light of early daybreak, when the world was new and clean-looking, they broke out beyond their own world of sage and cleared-land, into the high, sloping country of a great watershed that ran southward and eastward for a hundred miles and more.

"Hyar! Hyar, boys!"

It was the bareheaded man with the shaggy blond hair. He was sitting his horse and waving them in towards him. Forge loped over swiftly. Waite Hefner went slower, as though uneager to see what they all knew the bareheaded man had discovered.

"There they are. Indian tracks. Unshod horse. Looks like they were slowin' down."

Forge looked once and turned away curtly. "Let's go," he said, lifting the sorrel horse into an easy lope, watching the wide swath left by the raiders.

They went ahead making better time until the land showed more pronounced breaks, and after that Forge reined up once and waited for the others.

"Waite — you and I will push on. The rest of you favour your animals. We don't know how long this is going to last. If we come onto anything one of us'll ride back. Another thing: A couple of you boys take turns hanging back. The men from Sageland ought to be making time towards us. If you see 'em, there should be one man back along the trail to lead them on in."

They kept on riding and, except for that single stop, they weren't together again until they had crossed the Arkansas River.

The Comanche trail led them in a half-moon swing across the foothills, bearing southward. Waite Hefner seemed to understand the significance of the route. He reined up on a hill of brush and studied the lay of the land south and west of them.

"They're goin' home, Forge. Sure as the devil they're goin' right on through. I figgered they'd do a little more raidin', but from the looks of their trail now, I'd say they're goin' straight back where they came from."

Forge looked out over the land-fall below them. "Where's home?" he asked. "Looks to me like they could be anywhere down there."

"Maybe. I reckon though that they're goin' south into New Mexico."

"That means at least three more days before we can hope to find them."

Hefner looked over at Forge. "We'd better find them before they get home," he said. "If we don't I've got a notion it'll be too late."

Forge pushed the sorrel horse down off the knoll with a word. He understood.

The men were out of food. A few had grabbed up whatever they could glean back at the Knowlton place. Of water there was plenty. Hardly a day passed that they didn't cross at least two creeks, but that didn't help their hunger any. Then, one dark night in a dry-camp when their spirits were at their lowest, a lone rider came skittering down a slope towards them on a powerful black horse. Asa Knowlton.

He was haggard, armed to the teeth and more silent, taciturn, than ever. Forge recognised him without friendliness or unfriendliness. He waited. Knowlton hobbled his horse and clanked up to their foodless bivouac. He addressed Forge without any preliminaries.

"The rest are about seven miles behind me, Windsor. We picked up the man you had hanging back about sundown." He squatted, his big bulk making one more shapeless blob against the watery background.

"Where are they?"

Forge shrugged. "South of here somewhere. We haven't seen them yet."

Knowlton's big head swung a little, as though he would be able to pierce the gloom and the miles with his glance. "Do any of you know this country?"

"Waite here, does; passably well, anyway."

Knowlton swung his glance back to the Texan. "Where do you think they're going?"

128

"Guessing, I'd say they've got a camp out on the plains somewhere. Like I told Forge — I think the best thing's to try our dangdest to get real close to 'em before they get back home. If we don't, our chances of — succeeding — will be darn near done for."

"Then," Knowlton said, looking back at Forge, "why don't we ride on right now?"

"The horses," Forge said dourly. "They've had too much hard use. They've got to be rested a little."

Knowlton considered this for a long moment of silence, then he stood up. "I'll go ahead," he said stiffly.

Forge looked up at him. The old antagonism was stirring to life within him. "What good'll that do? If you find *them* it'll only let them know they're being trailed. If they find *you*, Knowlton, you'll never see daylight again."

Hefner said, "How about the little girl? If you give us away by riding down there alone, they'll brain her sure as the devil."

Knowlton ignored them and their logic. "You've been five days now," he said, "and we're no closer than when you started. For all any of us know Maria may be dead by now. Have any of you a steel mirror?"

Forge wondered but said nothing. Waite Hefner looked puzzled and annoyed. "Steel mirror? What for?"

"So I can signal back to you if I find them. You'll be joined by Luther Windsor's party by then and can come over my trail on the double."

"Oh." Hefner was mollified and asked among the listening men, but no one had such an article. Forge thought it over. The idea was sound enough.

"Take some dirt and burnish your belt-buckle or the cheekpiece of your bit, Knowlton. That ought to work. I think you're making a fool play though. It'd be better if we all rode after them."

"Like you've been doing?" Knowlton said unpleasantly. "I disagree. When you're fighting an enemy, go after him. Give him no rest."

"This is different," Forge said quickly. "If they didn't have the child we probably wouldn't even be here. As it is, if we spook them we'll get just exactly what we're trying to avoid. A killing."

There would have been others in the argument too, but Knowlton turned on his heel and went back to his horse.

They listened to the animal's shod hooves until even the echoes were gone. No one spoke. Forge was angry. The night hid most of it from the silent, squatting men with their unclean-looking faces and their sunken eyes. He should have forbidden Knowlton from going. The knowledge came late, though.

Waite Hefner sighed and stretched his long, thin legs out in front of him and stared at his toes. "He'll never find them, but I'll lay you odds they find him. We shouldn't have let him go. They'll figure one white man'll be leading more white men."

Forge stared into the night. He heard but paid no heed. He was angry at himself for letting Knowlton jeopardize their chances like this. It took an effort to force his mind back to their present situation. He said, "No, I should've made him stay. Ordered him to." But even as he said it he knew, as did the others, that

130

without force and a lot of it, the order never would have been obeyed. "The fool," he added thoughtlessly. "Waite — take a horse and go hunt up the posse from Sageland. Bring them on down here. There's only one thing to do now and that's to follow Knowlton."

"You're right," the bareheaded man said after a long study of the ground at his feet. "We got to. Maybe we can steal a march on 'em. Thing is — it'll play hob with the horses. They're already tucked up, but if it'll put us up onto them heathen, why I don't allow we'll need horse-guts afterward — for a while anyway."

Hefner sided in. "Might be a good idea at that, Forge. We want to fetch 'em a cropper before they get back to their camp, don't we?"

"I reckon," Forge said, standing up, feeling the old, pointless restlessness churning within him. "But this is forcing things and I'm not sure that's the right thing to do."

"No choice now," Hefner said succinctly, then he grunted resignedly and arose, ran a grimy hand over his beard stubble and swore. "I'm as sick of that horse as he is of me," he said. "Well — I'll go find the others and bring 'em in."

Forge walked away from the others.

He watched the eerie light of the sickle moon worry at the dark places, contending with the somnolent shadows and failing to make headway against them. A man could go to the lonely places in the night with his thoughts and be welcome.

He found a small hillock with a wide buffalo trail up it and climbed unthinkingly towards the eminence. The way was steep and the shale underfoot slippery. He breathed hard and from that self-imposed discomfort drew a bitter pleasure. Higher, he came across a huge boulder worn smooth and shiny from the generations of lice-bothered beasts that had rubbed and scratched and grunted in ecstasy over its hardness. There was a tawny smell up there. A gamey, wild odour, that went with the spot.

He stopped, breathing heavily, and leaned back on the rock with his thoughts jumbled and vivid. Weariness made him less inclined towards his usual coldness of mind. He remembered a lot of things. The flood of memories came down behind his eyes. Snatches of sentences CarrieLee had said.

"I don't care whether you believe it or not . . . Our daughter . . . a man I wouldn't want to know, anyway . . . Don't let them hurt her, Forge . . ."

Aloud, but softly, he said, "Lies. All lies. She said it for her own purpose. And Knowlton — the fool." He turned and glared at the old boulder. Asa Knowlton! He had a moment of blind hatred when he felt like cursing the big emigrant's gullibility. "Someone should have warned him about her. No; it's better this way. Someday he'll find out. You can't hide things like that forever. They have a way of coming out. Knowlton'll get a jolt when it comes out, too."

But he didn't enjoy his thoughts. Didn't like the way his mind was dumping them out with a droplet of savage hatred in each one. He turned and leaned on the rock and stared at the ground where the moon-wash was.

What if it was true? That was in '56 . . . She would be four years old. It shocked him, thinking that, but what if it was? He recalled what the Knowlton boy had said. "Five or six — maybe seven — I don't know." He almost smiled in his cold, hard way. A boy wouldn't know; wouldn't care, really. A little girl could be three or six, a boy wouldn't care.

He balled his fists and crossed his arms across his chest. It had been in May. That was a vivid memory all these years. May, 1856. If it was his daughter, then she'd have been born about February of '57. This was '61. That'd make her four — close to five because fall was here again. Five years old. He turned swiftly and went farther up the trail and mumbled aloud, "I don't believe it!"

From the top of the little hillock there was a flat, brooding darkness northward in an angling way, where the heavy shadows of the huge mountains rose tier after purpling tier, cutting across the bosom of upland plains.

He stood there feeling less warmth than he had felt down in the unmarked camp. It was a solitary, gloomy place. The buffalo trace angled on by it and out of sight, northward. He hunkered, rocking a little back and forth nursing his bitterness and his memories. It was like torture, too, the way his mind went back to CarrieLee's smile, her warmth and passion that could inundate, suffocate, a person. The firmness of her, the fragrance — even the steady, unflinching way her grey eyes had of looking into you, and suddenly he couldn't hide the fact that he hated himself for the things he had said to her that time, in his office.

He swore in a sing-song voice and closed his eyes tightly to force out the memories that were acid in his mind and heart.

He opened his eyes, got up and stood wide-legged. Five years old — a little under, really — and in the hands of stinking carrion eaters with about as much heart as wolves. He turned his head a little. The moist moonlight fell across his face. He couldn't know how wild and fierce he looked with all the hatred of a powerful, passionate personality shining out of his blue eyes.

He was standing like that when he saw the light far south of him — so far beyond the grasp of his immediate thoughts that he stared at it a full minute before its significance seeped past the other things in his mind. Then he frowned and concentrated on it. A reddish light, glowing with dazzling intensity, but far away. Twisting up, growing and swaying like . . .

"Good God! They're down there! They've hit another ranch!"

He wasn't conscious of running until he fell and skinned his palms in the flinty shale. His lungs were pumping hot air that tasted like creosote bush, the way it burned, when he stormed into camp and saw the host of horsemen standing by their mounts there. Their numbers startled him. It wasn't just the original nine. There must've been thirty of them, at least.

"Forge, we've been waiting for you."

"Luther!" He went closer, saw the strange expression jump into his brother's face at sight of him. Saw the way Waite Hefner was staring, mouth agape. He didn't bother to alter his expression.

"Lute — they're down there on the plains south and west of us. There's a big fire down there. I saw it from a hill behind us here. It's another ranch I'll bet my life." He turned towards Hefner. "Get my horse, Waite. Let's go!"

Hefner held out a pair of split reins with a rueful and resigned smile. "He's here. I figgered you'd want him."

They rode out of the little upland camp almost forty strong. A formidable force heavily enough armed to stand a siege or lay one down. Grim men without elation in their expressions — without mercy either.

Forge motioned Waite to go ahead and lay out a trail for them, then he rode a little apart, beside Luther. The older brother's face, in the moonlight, was set in an obstinate, hard way. None of Luther's usual gentleness showed.

"Lute; Knowlton went on."

"I know. Hefner told us. That wasn't very smart."

Forge shifted a little in his saddle and made no attempt to deny it. "We'll come up to him," he said. "He won't get far, it's too cussed dark. He doesn't know the country. Besides — from the looks of that fire, Lute, I'd say it's a good fifteen miles out."

Luther rode like the rest of them, in absolute silence; moving with the rhythm of his horse, preoccupied. Forge noticed it and lapsed into a reverie of his own for a while, but the memories came back more easily now.

He urged his horse away from his brother as though to ride on ahead. Luther's voice suddenly called him back.

"Forge."

He reined up, turned a little, waiting. "Yes?"

"I've got something to tell you."

The way his brother said it made Forge's innards tighten into a hard knot. He knew instinctively what it was about. "It'll keep," he said tightly, resenting Luther's interference, lifting the reins again.

"No it won't!" Luther exclaimed harshly, startling Forge with his tone and the quick stare that went with it. This wasn't like Luther at all. "Ride out with me a ways."

They moved at right angles to the silent band of horsemen. Everywhere the moonlight struck it was thrown back in reflection from steel butt-plates and pistol cylinders, from laden bandoleers of cartridges and wicked looking belt-knives.

Luther went wide of the others, then swung southward. Forge rode in close to him, knee to knee. The land was dropping away abruptly. Neither of them spoke until they had navigated the steepness and were travelling over flat country once more. Forge looked along the skyline for the flash of the distant flames. He couldn't find them but it didn't matter. He knew about where they were, just as he knew about what they'd find when they got to them.

"Forge?"

"Go ahead, Lute," he said gruffly.

"We had a little excitement in town the night we got word of the attack at Knowlton's. In fact, it broke up the meeting at my place. Five of the men from the ranches north of town caught a horsethief red-handed. They brought him into town and sent word to me at the house. They knew we were all up there."

"So you hung him," Forge said, lifting his glance to the horizon again, searching for the flames that weren't there.

"No. We almost did though. I talked them into locking him up for a while. Until this mess is over with. Until you've talked to him at least."

"Why?"

"Well, he asked for me by name, Forge. He sent word he wanted to see me before they strung him up. I went down to the jailhouse with the rest of the men, and had a long talk with him. Privately, I mean." Luther was looking straight ahead. His fixed glance was on the distant, moving back of Waite Hefner, who had three other men riding beside him a quarter of a mile or so ahead.

"He wanted a drink. I gave him one. Then he told me the strangest story I've ever heard. He's a drunk all right. I won't deny that. A drunk and worse. He looks like he's all eaten out inside, too. Burnt out, maybe. But that's neither here nor there."

"No," Forge said, looking oddly at his brother. "That's not why you asked me to ride over here with you, is it?"

"No. I've been trying to think of a way to start. Well — I'll just jump in, Forge."

"Go ahead," Forge urged him, wondering more than ever.

137

"He told me he'd been studying over horse herds around Sageland and stumbled across a woman he recognised. It was CarrieLee Knowlton. He'd known her before. In fact, he said she'd been his old pardner's wife over in Abilene. His pardner's name was Mark Belleau. Later, I went over to the constable's office and looked through the old wanted posters. There was nothing there, but that doesn't mean anything. There was no time to check the rest of his story, but I'll do it when I get back.

"What was the rest of it, Lute?"

"He told me about this Belleau. About CarrieLee and her daughter. It isn't a very pretty story."

"I don't reckon it is," Forge said. Dark blood was filling his face. The weak light hid it from Luther.

"This man's name is Stan Stryker. He said CarrieLee's husband was a horsethief too. He was killed in an ambush near Salina. Stryker says that CarrieLee's daughter was not Belleau's child and that Belleau knew it. That he deliberately went on this raid when he was drunk and nothing Stryker could say would make him wait until he was fit to take the chance. There was a posse waiting for them — Stryker says he found out later other horsethieves had been operating down there and the countryside was an armed camp, but that night he didn't know it. Anyway — when the shooting stopped Belleau was dead and Stryker just barely got away with his life. Forge — Stryker said Belleau's being drunk like that caused his death. He says the drunkenness was CarrieLee's fault — because of her child."

138

The blow was a hard one. Forge took it erect in his saddle with his eyes as still, as hushed-looking and dark, as the night itself. Luther was watching him, but he couldn't see the extent of Forge's reaction. The light was too soft, too vague.

"CarrieLee didn't know her husband was a horsethief." Then Luther made the only personal remark he ever made. "She was only a kid, those days, Forge. A country kid left loose in a town like Abilene. Well — anyway — do you want to hear the rest of it?"

"Why not?" Forge said distantly.

"This Stryker said when old Tim hit the town he got wall-eyed drunk. I believe that, too; I didn't know the Dolans as well as you did, but I knew him that well from seeing him at the Fontaine camp-meetings years back. He'd get pretty drunk and leave CarrieLee foot loose. You've seen that happen, Forge. This Belleau married her in Abilene under similar circumstances."

"Lute — did he say when her daughter was born?"

"Yes. He said it happened sometime after the first of the year in '57."

"February of '57," Forge said.

Luther threw him a look then he turned away. "There isn't a lot more to tell," he said. I got the constable's word he wouldn't let anything happen to Stryker until you and I got back from this chase. Then you can talk to him."

Forge nodded his head shortly. "Yes, I'd like to," he said. There was a hardness to the words.

139

Luther looked over at him quickly. His blue eyes were shades darker in the gloom. "You don't think it's the truth, do you?"

"Don't I?" Forge said bitterly. "How the hell do I know? How do you know Lute? How could anyone ever know whether he's a liar — and CarrieLee's another one — or not?"

"It's the truth all right," Luther said in his old, quiet way. "It isn't lies and it isn't coincidence, I can tell you that right now. It's much too close to what we know, to be a pack of lies. I didn't have any time to check it, Forge, but I'll make you a bet. I'll bet you everything I own against what you own, that Stryker's not lying in the parts of his story that matter."

Forge swung his head. His eyes were hot-looking. "You're pretty well convinced, Lute."

Luther made an abrupt, angry wag with his head. "Think it over, Forge. How else would Stryker know *all* about it? How else would he know the dates and everything — if he wasn't there? Why would he tell such a straightforward story?"

"To save his neck," Forge said. "That's why. I'd do the same and so would you."

"You're wrong. He wasn't that afraid of being hung. The law had him locked up and was guarding him with shotguns when we all got down there. If they'd been going to lynch him, they wouldn't have taken him to the jailhouse, Forge. Use your head."

"You'll have to do better than that, Lute," Forge said. "There's no question about some of it being the truth, but the parts that count — with me, anyway — leave me a long way from being convinced."

"All right, Forge," Luther said. "All right. I'll tell you the thing that clinched it for me even though I said I wouldn't. When they searched him at the constable's office he had over two hundred dollars on him. I asked him where he got it. He said CarrieLee had given it to him. Said he'd hidden out at the Knowlton place until he'd seen Asa ride out, then slipped down there and got it from her to get out of the country on."

Forge was calmer. His glance at Luther was sardonic. "That all, Lute?" he said in an ironic way.

"Not quite. I went up to your rooms in the hotel where she was and took her aside and asked her bluntly if she'd given a man two hundred dollars. She said no, she'd given a man named Stryker three hundred dollars. That was close enough. He'd spent some of it, naturally." Luther's eyes narrowed. "Then, Forge — she made me promise solemnly never to tell a living soul she'd done that — and especially, *never to tell you*."

Forge said nothing. Luther rode along beside him for a while before he spoke again. His words were slow and bitter, then. "Make a lie out of that," he said, and spurred away.

Forge's thoughts were like wet ashes — grey and sticky — a morass of doubts. She'd said, "I don't care what you think . . ." She'd meant every word of it. She *didn't* care; didn't *want* him to be convinced that Maria was his daughter. That hadn't been a lie then. It hadn't been a snare set to trap him at all. More of it would be true too; it had to be.

141

He rode apart from the band of heavily armed, stony-faced men, lost in a crumbling world of doubts. Up ahead Luther called out something he couldn't make out. He lifted his head and looked. There was a dying brilliance they could all see plainly now, against a backdrop of the horizon's black, bitter gloom.

What wrenched him away from his thoughts was a shout from far ahead. A yell that echoed down across the stillness with overtones of horror in it.

Instinctively Forge kicked out his horse. He came up abreast of Luther and the two of them led the armed men from Sageland in an easy gallop towards the sound.

They saw Waite Hefner and a few others when they were limned against the firelight that wasn't more than a half mile ahead of them. Most of the possemen dismounted when they swung up, but some were silhouetted starkly in their saddles. Forge reined down to a walk and rode in closer. He had a feeling . . .

It was Asa Knowlton. They knew him by his size. There was little else to identify him by. His skull was a scarlet jelly, his guns and part of his clothing were gone. There was no sign of his big black horse. He was face up and sprawled. There was a shifting movement across his vacant stare where the distant firelight reflected.

Hefner was on his knees by the body when the others came up. He arose and shot a long glance at Forge. "Arrers," he said. "Three of 'em. He never knew what hit him." He held up two headless shafts he had broken off. There was one vertical line of black paint and a

142

matching line of red paint, down each arrow-shaft. "Comanche arrers."

Forge didn't dismount but Luther did. There was no point to it. He watched his brother walk over and stand above the dead man, looking down as though to clarify a doubt that might linger in his mind.

Forge raised his glance and let it stray to the glowing embers in the near distance. There was more red than yellow in the flames. They were dying. He stiffened a little in the saddle and said, "Lute; I'm going on."

The older man turned slowly. "All right," he said. "I'll keep back a few hands. We'll bury him."

Forge led the rest of the riders towards the gutted ranch. It was the same thing over again, with some variations. They found three dead Indians strewn before what had once been a ranch house. There were no survivors. Forge guessed they must have perished in the flames. The bars of a pole-corral were down. That held his attention more than anything else did. It took no great knowledge of tracking and sign-reading to understand that. The raiders had stampeded the rancher's horses across the yard. It made Forge groan inwardly. Fresh horses. They might never get close to the Indians now.

"One's cooked," someone said close to him. He turned and saw the bareheaded man gazing at an Indian who had been killed close to the house. "Fried him, dang near," the man said dispassionately.

There was no sign of life anywhere around the place. Forge stalked wearily through the fierce heat that was ebbing and flowing fitfully from the dying blaze. It was

143

a waste of time, staying there. He saw that at once. When Luther rode up later at a stiff trot with a half dozen men around him, Forge stopped walking and waited. There was only rubble and ruin. Luther looked down into a haggard face.

"Any use in staying here?"

"None. Even less here than at Knowlton's. I'll get my horse."

They struck out with the flames backgrounding them. The grim assistance of the unnatural light afforded them the means to find the Comanche trail again with no trouble. It was westerly now, more than southerly. Hefner rode in close to Forge, swearing softly. Forge glanced over at him. "What's the matter?"

"Nothing new," Hefner said. "The same thing. I'd like to get just one shot at them. Just one."

"You will," Forge said stonily. "If the horses hold out."

"I don't know," Hefner said. "They've got fresh animals. That makes a heap of difference."

Forge said nothing. It was useless to talk about it; they all knew the condition of their mounts. His own — the blaze-faced sorrel — was still strong and moving willingly, but anyone with half an eye could see the tucked-up gauntness of his flanks. None of their horses would last very much longer without a long rest and a lot of feed. He turned back towards the Texan again.

"Have you ever been in this country we're going through now?"

"Yes," Waite Hefner said. "I campaigned this once, over here."

"Do you know where there are any big ranches close by? Places where we could get fresh horses?"

Hefner's short laugh was low and unpleasant. "There's only Injuns down here. Injuns and graves and burnt out places. Any horses we find in this country — we'll have to kill Injuns off the tops of them to get 'em."

Forge thought of that for a moment then he reined away from the Texan and went down the line in search of his brother. Luther was riding alone, his head low on his chest.

"Lute; they aren't too far ahead. Maybe two — three hours of hard riding."

Luther looked up briefly and nodded. His face was grey and slack-muscled looking. Sad and melancholy. He said nothing at all.

"If we ride like we're doing now, they'll get away. They've got fresh horses. If we ever do find them at this rate, it may not be until they're back at their village."

"I know all that," Luther said wearily.

"Then let's gamble, Lute. Let's push our animals for all we can get out of them and see if we can't close with them. Maybe our horses'll hold out — maybe they won't. It's a long chance but it's our only one, as I see it."

Luther was looking at his brother with an unblinking stare. He said, "Are you willing to do that, Forge?"

Forge understood. "Yes," he said. "I can't see any other way. They will know by now — from Knowlton — that we're behind them."

"Not necessarily," Luther said. "They may have thought he was a lone rider attracted by the flames.

145

They'd hardly expect one man out of a band to ride down on them like that."

That might be right too, but secretly, in the darkest place of his heart, Forge didn't believe Maria was still alive. Not after all the blood-letting the Comanche bucks had moved through. He knew how unpredictable, how thoroughly savage and cruel they were. What he wanted now was to close with them; get in where the men from Sageland could put an end to this wearying, exhausting pursuit that was wearing them all out, men and horses alike.

"Lute," he said. "We can't keep this up. Come daylight, our horses will be just about done for. One more day under this sun and the men won't be in any better shape. The horses are starved and so are the men. It's got to be ended one way or the other. If we *don't* push on, we'll be licked anyway. Another thing, Lute — if the Indians see us after sunup — which they'll be sure to do since this is open country — they'll streak away on those fresh horses and we won't be able to get near them."

"And Maria?"

Forge looked stonily at his brother. "After daylight, Lute — if she's still with them — they'll lay her out on the trail where we'll find her. You know that."

"I reckon I do," Luther said.

Forge rode back where the men were bunched up, stopped them with an up-flung arm and explained what he and Luther had talked about. Waite Hefner and one or two others were grimly silent but their faces spoke volumes. The balance of the riders were impressed with

146

Forge's logic — his prestige had risen meteorically since they had seen him under the present light — and they were ready to use up what little reserve strength their horses possessed in this final rush.

When they were all moving briskly forward again, Waite Hefner rode stirrup with Forge. He was smoking with long, deep inhalations, using tobacco as a substitute for food. "I'll take a dozen or so and go on ahead," he said. "'Signal with a gunshot if I stumble onto anything — otherwise I'll send back a man."

Forge nodded in silence and watched them lope ahead. Deep down inside he was frightened.

CHAPTER
SEVEN

Comanches!

By the time the sky was lightening the Sageland men had drunk their fill at a creek, smoked for breakfast, and mounted up for the last push onward.

They were riding across a trail that was fifty feet wide and laden with dun-dust that looked like ochre in the soft light. Eyes that flinched away from any glare were swollen and red with fatigue, but there was still resolve in them. No eagerness, just tiredness and determination.

Forge rode stonily, alone and apart from the others, watching the paleness come into the sky. Once, he swung to look back at the horizon. A weak blueness was there pushing against the soft under-belly of the night. He turned forward and looked at the country up ahead. It was rolling grassland. The summer had dried it out but, he thought instinctively, it was good land. He looked at the Sageland men and their horses and wagged his head pityingly. Just about finished, both of them.

Far ahead Waite Hefner — Texan — was outlined briefly on a grassy upthrust. Off to his right was a long ridge of sage and scrub brush. Apparently Hefner had just ridden back from that ridge. Forge watched the

Texan and the little clutch of riders with him. They went out of sight over the crest of the grassy knoll. It was as though they were going downstairs — bobbing up and down beyond the sheer drop-off until he couldn't see them any more. He shook his head and rubbed his eyes with stiff knuckles. He saw Luther and began to edge his horse around the body of riders until he was up beside him.

His brother looked more worn out and weary than any of the others. He thought it was because Lute hadn't had any exercise — had been loafing too much — these last few years. There was no disapproval in the thought, just recognition of a fact that stood out now where it hadn't before.

"Lute? You feel all right?"

Luther lifted his head and affected a thin smile. "I've felt better," he said. "Too sleep-drunk right now to remember when, but I have." He struggled upright in his saddle and squinted at Forge's appearance in the dismal light. "You're no beauty, you know."

Forge forced a smile at the flimsy humour. "I reckon not," he said. "If we don't find 'em pretty doggoned soon we'll all be in a bad way. 'Can't keep this up."

"We'll find them," Luther said. There was conviction in his words.

Forge studied his face for a moment before he spoke again. "You're that sure, are you?"

Luther held up a dyed, shortened horse's tail. "This sure," he said.

Forge's surprise was in his voice, high and abrupt. "Where the devil did you get that thing?"

"Back a ways. About ten miles from the burnt out ranch. It was on an Indian shield. Hunter's shield, if I remember all I used to know about them. Buffalo-neck rawhide with horse's tails dyed and fastened around the edge of it. Big medicine shield," Luther said scoffingly. "Heap big medicine shield."

"Just a shield? No buck — loose horse — anything else?"

"Just the shield with a bullethole through it. I reckon the warrior must've tossed it aside in disgust. His medicine didn't turn the bullet so the shield had failed him — lost its power. There wouldn't be a loose horse anyway. They took Asa Knowlton's black — they'd take this man's horse too — even if he died on the trail, which I doubt. I've been watching for a cairn — haven't seen one yet."

"They ride horses back and forth over graves when they're out raising hell like this."

Luther shrugged as though it didn't matter. "I reckon," he said. "Anyway — this is all I need to know we're going right."

The bareheaded blond man had ridden close to Forge's left side. He was leaning forward in his saddle. A brush of fingers across Forge's arm brought his attention to the newcomer.

"Up there — it's Hefner."

Forge and Luther both turned in the indicated direction and peered through the dawn light. The Texan was sitting his horse on the grassy knoll again. He had his hat over his head in both hands. Forge spoke so softly the other two men didn't hear him.

150

"He's found them. He sees them."

Others had noticed. The possemen slowed, then stopped, a few spoke, most did not, but all of them had seen Waite Hefner up there and knew what he was signalling down to them about.

Forge heard their hushed voices without heeding them. He heard the sound of metal against leather, the slithering whispers of guns being withdrawn from holsters and carbine-boots. With those noises came a gorge of iciness inside him. Miraculously, his weariness dropped away.

"Luther; watch the men here. We can't have anything spoiling this."

He boosted the lagging sorrel into a sloppy lope and went up the incline towards Waite Hefner. The distance wasn't more than a half mile but his mount laboured over it like it was much farther. The Texan had his shapeless hat back on and a rusty flush to his face. His eyes were alive through a sheen of exhaustion.

"What'd you see, Waite?"

"Injuns. Comanches." Hefner waved a vague hand backwards with little thought of accurate direction. "A big party of them, Forge. If that kid saw only twenty then he didn't see 'em all. They're in camp. Must've rode most of the night. Looks like more'n a hundred horses in their pony-herd. I'd say they've hit more'n two ranches from the look of that herd."

"How many of them?"

"Can't rightly say. It's danged hard to make 'em out and I didn't want to get any closer. They've got dogs with 'em. Comanches do that; take cussed dogs that'll

151

bark at the smell of anything strange, and go crazy when they scent-up a white man."

"How many would you guess, then?"

"Maybe close to sixty, Forge. Hell — there may be eighty or a hundred for all I know. Like I said — you can't rightly tell. Anyway — I left a couple of the boys up there lyin' behind the brush, watching them." Hefner stopped speaking. His right cheek bulged with tobacco he had gotten from some chewer. He waited for Forge to speak.

"How close can we get before they guess we're around?"

"Half a mile, I'd say. Comanches're plenty coyote. They won't camp anywhere but in the middle of a plain, if they can help it." Waite turned and nodded up at the brushy ridge. "We can go up as far as that knoll where the boys are lyin', but beyond that they can see us. We'd have to ride near a quarter of a mile out in the open to reach them."

Hefner faced Forge and shook his head gravely. "That's too far. It wouldn't take a buck a tenth of that time to grab up the little girl and knock her brains out on a rock."

Forge turned in his saddle and watched the main body of possemen coming up the incline behind him. They were bunched up close. Luther was ahead, the bareheaded blond man was right behind him. He was carrying his pistol in his fist. The steely daylight shone off it moistly.

"What you want to do, Forge?" Waite Hefner asked.

"Wait a little," Forge answered dismounting. He moved around so he could study the land ahead of them. There was a downward slope, a wide valley, then another hill even higher than the grassy knoll and across from that lay the sagebrush ridge.

"Is that where you left your men?"

"Yeah. In among the brush clumps up there."

"And the Comanches are down the far side and out on a plain?"

"That's right. It's another valley like this one below us, only a heap wider. Maybe five miles wide."

Forge heard the creak of leather as Luther and the rest of the band dismounted behind him. He swept a long, squinted glance at the northern hills. It was apparent they were coming again to brush country; there were even trees and tall, gaunt stalks of chaparral and manzanita among the crowded sage clumps, northward. His head moved slowly as he studied the flow of scrub growth. "Waite? Does that brush run solid along the north foothills, up there?"

"Yeah. As far as I could see it does, Forge."

Luther edged in closer leading his horse. He walked as though his legs pained him; flat-footed, knee-sprung. "Where are they, Forge?"

"Over that brushy hill across the way from us. Half mile or so out in a big valley the other side."

"Too far," Luther said promptly.

"Maybe." Forge faced his brother. "They aren't greenhorns, Lute. They pick those camps for their open country. Anyone slips up on a Comanche accomplishes

153

something to brag about. I've got an idea though — see what you think of it."

Hefner growled behind Forge. He turned like a striking snake and until that moment didn't know how tightly wound he was inside. "What is it, Waite?"

"Yonder — that feller making a cigarette. Their dogs'll smell that a mile off."

Luther turned and spoke to the man, saw his chagrin and faced back towards Forge again. "All right," he said. "I'm listening."

Forge didn't meet his brother's gaze. "I'll ride down alone —"

"Wait a minute," Hefner said quickly. "You wouldn't get past the first buck. I *know* Comanches. They'll gut you like an antelope and wonder what you came for — afterwards."

"Maybe," Forge said without looking at the Texan. "Lute — I'll ride down and try to talk to them. If we all bust over that ridge they're going to kill her if she's still with 'em."

"And," Hefner persisted, "If you ride down there alone, they'll kill *you*."

Forge looked his exasperation when he swung on the Texan. Luther saw it and, knowing his brother's sharp tongue, broke in before Forge could speak. "It looks like about the only way, at that. Either way there's a risk. We know what they'll do if we storm them across a mile or so of open country. This way it may make them wonder — hold them back a little. It's a chance."

"Yeah," the Texan said dourly. "The same chance a rattler's got in a ranchyard."

154

Forge ignored Hefner. "Lute — Waite says there's brush all along the north rim up there. Take the posse up there as high as you have to get, to be well hidden in the sage. Whatever you do don't take any chances on being seen. Watch me from up there. Use your head after that. If they're hostile — try anything you can think of that'll put you among 'em before they can hurt her. If I can palaver with them, don't do anything until I get back. But whatever you do don't take any chances on being seen — or smelled — from their camp. You might even split up the boys and try for a surround, I don't know. That'll be up to you after I go down there."

"If they get their wind up," Hefner said shrewdly, "they'll head out westward again."

"All right," Forge said. "If that's what they do, Lute, get as far west of them as you can and still be hidden, then, when they strike out, hit them with everything you've got. By then I'll either be a coup or a prisoner. Anyway — keep an eye on me and try to figure out what to do from what happens when I go down there."

"Amen," someone said quietly.

Luther was scowling. "We should leave someone back here in case they break back up this way."

"I'll stay," Waite Hefner said. "Give me a few men and I'll stay." Luther raised his eyebrows and Forge nodded. "Good enough. There won't be much danger back here I don't expect. Anyway, if they head west again that'll put Waite behind them. He can bust after them and that ought to help like the devil. Make them think they're facing a regular army of vigilantes behind and in front both. They'll break up and run for it."

Luther said slowly, "We'll be against pretty big odds."

With an impatient frown Forge said, "What's the difference? You've got just so many Comanches and there're just so many of us. Either way we'll have to face everything they've got. This way — if we can surprise 'em — at least it'll shake their confidence."

The Texan was ruminating his cud thoughtfully. With grudging reluctance he held his peace. Forge didn't look at Luther again. He turned and mounted the sorrel horse and rode away from the silent men on the grassy knoll without once looking back.

Crossing the narrow valley below he had time to reconsider. He was doing a desperate and foolhardy thing, but if there was another way to accomplish his ends he didn't think of it.

Following faint game trails he wound up the far slope towards the sagebrush ridge. Nearing the top he saw men shuntling towards him. He reined up just short of the skyline and spoke to them.

"Boys, stay right where Waite put you. My brother's bringing most of the crew up here right now. Waite'll stay back where he is with a few others."

A man with sunken, red-rimmed eyes, asked, "What are you up to?"

"I'm going to ride down and palaver with them."

Forge knew the men would erupt into vigorous protests and they did. He sat patiently waiting for the storm to subside, then told them, "Don't worry about me. You just do your part and don't let the devils see you."

156

He pushed the sorrel horse on past them and closed his mind to the hoarsely whispered predictions they threw in his wake, crested the eminence and saw the Comanche encampment down below.

There weren't any tepis; from that he knew it was strictly a fast-moving war party. There were huddled shapes, dark and indistinct in the pinkness of the new day, that he knew were Indians squatting with their backs to him — to the sun — over by the large herd of horses. Cooking fires sent up crooked tendrils of smoke. He nudged the sorrel horse and rode him down the slope and out of the brush into plain sight. He was slouched in the saddle.

The camp was hastily made, he could see that as he got closer. There were mounds of saddlery, of long, wicked-looking warrior lances with drooping feathers and bits of gaudy cloth tied to them, standing at random among the carelessly flung down sacks of plunder and sleeping robes. Blankets and personal paraphernalia were scattered indiscriminately wherever a warrior had slept.

In two separate spots were upright warrior lances imbedded in the ground. Mid-way down each lanceshaft hung a warrior's shield. Oval, very thick Medicine Shields, each bearing the heraldic emblems of the man who owned them. There, he knew, would be the leaders.

He tried to count the Comanches as he rode towards them. It was impossible. Someone cried out at sight of him and the camp was boiling with activity before the echo had died away. Even the drowsing, hunched over

157

horse-guards jumped erect and spun towards him, facing into the sun and shielding their eyes with their hands, watching the astonishing spectacle of a single white man on a tuckered sorrel horse riding towards their camp.

Forge smelled the food while he was still two rifleshot lengths away. It made his stomach growl. He sniffed and thought it was probably horsemeat — but it was meat and it was cooked. He had been riding so long with emptiness where his stomach was that he had almost forgotten what cooking meat smelled like. Now, understandably, food loomed as important as his reception.

The Comanches were standing motionless, staring. Every one of them was armed; not a few had rifles and carbines but the majority had short, thick little war bows. None made a hostile move until he was well within bow range, then many raised their weapons and took aim.

That was the first terrible moment. It passed slowly, with all its agonising uncertainty dragged out until he was so close he could distinguish their features, and by then he knew they weren't going to shoot — yet.

He raised his hand high overhead and forward, palm out and fingers extended, to indicate that he came in peace. He rode that way for a hundred yards then he slowly dropped his arm and went right up to the foremost warriors, reined up and nodded very gravely at the crowd of dark, granite-looking fighting men.

One Comanche, taller than the rest with no facial hair at all — not even eyebrows, which gave him a

158

lizard-like appearance — said something that was absolutely unintelligible to Forge. He made an elaborate shrug and shook his head. Another warrior came forward and spoke in a mangled dialect of Spanish which Forge understood for what it was — Comanche-Spanish — but found equally unintelligible and he shook his head again. But when a wizened, older man made a brusque motion, he understood that all right, and complied.

Get down!

He did, dismounting and walking up to his horse's head. The Comanches crowded closer. One made an obscene gesture with a bared knife that drew a rippling laugh from some of the bystanders. Forge studied them. They were wary men whose eyes were never still. They flickered constantly like the eyes of wild animals that lived in an environment of constant peril.

The smell of their camp was pungent; their personal odours were no better. It came in part from their hair, which was worn long and in some cases braided, in others held away from their faces with an Apache-like sort of turbaned headband. Their eyes were muddy-looking, ranging from pitch black to light brown. Their stature was generally well below Forge's height but their breadth of chest and shoulder was in startling contrast to their bandy legs — as much from ricketts as from horseback riding — and two things particularly impressed Forge.

One was their very glaring and obvious hostility. The other was their sheer astonishment that he had ridden

159

boldly in among them when any fool could see they were a war party.

"Eat," he said suddenly. "Heap hungry." Trying it in Spanish he said, "Esa," almost the extent of his knowledge of that tongue, and directing it towards the wizened warrior who had himself spoken in Spanish.

The Indian understood but made no move to unbar Forge's path for a full two minutes of staring, then he wheeled away, crooked his hand and motioned for the white man to follow him.

The warriors trooped along, the initial shock past. They used gestures more than words. If a hand or arm motion would serve, they didn't speak at all. When their gestures needed amplification, the Comanches used the briefest, ugliest words Forge had ever heard. It was almost as though they lacked a vocabulary. They didn't; it was simply their way, to express themselves by movement — hand, arm, head, or body — rather than by sound. For a race that lived, fought, hunted and raided by stealth, this had particular advantages.

The old warrior led Forge to a grimy iron pot and waved a hand towards it. The smell was far less appetising when he was close, but it was still cooked meat. He bent a little and tested the stew with a finger. The Indians grinned when he pulled it back swiftly.

He took a knife from his belt and stabbed at a floating blob of tan-grey meat, skewered it with the first try and got another series of grins, drew it out and ate it. There was a wild taste to the stuff, almost as though the flavouring had been sage. It had. He knew the meat by its yellow tallow to be bear meat.

160

He ate four large chunks before he was conscious of a tall Indian standing across the kettle from him. Taller, a little lighter, more brooding and bitter and angry-eyed than the other bucks, this Comanche was fully clothed even under his blanket. Forge nodded at the man, who acted as though he hadn't seen, then finished eating and tucked his knife away but didn't forget to make circular motions over his stomach to indicate his pleasure and gratitude.

He knew by the thick silence that the tall Indian across from him was either the sole war-leader or the ranking one. Not a Comanche moved after the big fellow came up. Forge gazed at the man. He was wrapped in a filthy old blanket that looked as though it had been yanked from over a sleeping soldier. If so, Forge doubted that the soldier any longer had need of a blanket. The buck's hair was worn long, parted in the middle and each braid was encased in a beige coloured animal skin of some kind. He had on a hunting or war-shirt that Forge could see under the loosely-held blanket. He also wore full length britches that had once been the property of a white man. These were stained and greasy almost beyond belief, but the original colour must have once been dark blue.

This warrior's face was well formed and, while his companions were very dark — as much from exposure as from natural pigmentation — his face wasn't nearly as dark as theirs. Forge saw too, that his eyes were a lighter brown than most, but his full mouth, with a heavy and jutting underlip above the hard knurl of his

161

chin, was also more brutal and sullen than the lower features of his companions.

"Who you? Why you come-along?"

The English surprised Forge. It had heavy inflections to it but was easily understandable.

"You damn fool. *Big* damn fool. You come-along bad; you *get* bad!"

Forge had no trouble getting the drift of the Comanche's words. Forge had come at a bad time. He was going to be treated badly. He felt no misgiving he hadn't already experienced since arriving among the raiders. Making his face very solemn and without letting any more of the antagonism show than he could help, he answered in slow, sparse English.

"You raid long way off. You burn. You ride long trail away. I follow."

"Wh'-for? Who you name? Where you live-in?"

"I come to talk. My name's Forge Windsor. I live far out." Farge threw out his arm to indicate a vast distance.

The war-leader had no trouble pronouncing Forge but he couldn't get anywhere near Windsor and gave it up speedily. He repeated his earlier conviction about Forge. "You heap damn fool. We kill you."

Forge shrugged and said, "Not yet. No kill yet. We talk. We eat."

Forge's intimation of indifference over when he was killed drew low comments and sign-talk from the listening Indians. The wizened warrior spoke to the war-leader with his hand. Forge waited, studying the big leader. He had an inspired thought and reached

162

inside his coat, felt around for two limp cigars that were there, drew them out and offered one to the big Comanche. The warrior considered; none of the ire went out of his face even when he lowered his glance and sniffed at the cigar, took it and put it into his mouth.

Forge bit the end off his cigar, stooped, brushed at the dying fire for an ember and held out his own cigar for the tall Comanche to light up from. He deliberately held the cigar a little low so the warrior would have to bow towards him a trifle to light his own cigar. The Indian did, puffed with prodigous effort, then pulled back again and looked at Forge, still with no softening in his face.

"You come-along."

Forge followed the Indian, still leading his horse. The animal's lagging steps made him the object of scorn among the rugged riders of the southern plains. Their comments weren't hard to interpret. Right there, Forge learned to watch a Comanche's gestures and ignore his speech.

He went to where the tallest lance stood stark and barbaric in the morning freshness, following the war-leader. He gazed at the small shield hanging midway on the lance and gathered from the scalp-fringe around it that the Comanche leader was a mighty fighting man. Someone took the reins out of his hand. He relinquished them reluctantly but without showing it.

"You sit."

He sat, watching the big buck motion the others away. Among the scattered plunder and jumble of the camp he looked for some sign of a small white girl. There was nothing that looked promising as far as he could see, but the camp was sprawled over several acres. His heart sank nevertheless, almost devoid of hope, now.

"You-Foach," the Comanche said. "You be kill." The light brown eyes were cruel. The warrior pursed his lips, made a buzzing sound, formed his fingers to indicate a flying wasp and co-ordinated the moving fingers with the buzzing sound. Forge gathered what he meant and dimly, very dimly, he recalled having heard that the Comanche Indians were divided into sub-tribes, like all Plains Indians, and that one band, the most war-like of them all, was called Wasp-Comanche. Their own interpretation of the name wasp, however, indicated more the sting than the flight of the insect. (Wasp pronounced by the Comanches: Penane).

"Why you come-along, Foach? You tell now!"

Forge had a theory in his mind he'd perfected after he had ridden into the encampment. He tried it now when he said, "I come give you many horses. I come give you much food. Give you much cloth. Many cows." He paused, seeing the surprise and lowering suspicion in the pale-brown eyes across from him. "Make presents," he concluded.

"You white man; you no give-any. Why?"

"Make friends."

The big Indian made a loud grunt of contempt and looked down his nose. "No make good friend. White

164

man no come-along good friend. White man black heart — forked tongue. No good friend. No give-any. No good."

Forge deliberately hesitated before he spoke again. He held the Comanche's stare with his calm look, relaxing all his facial muscles to give an appearance of indifference, casualness. He at least had the raider wonderingly curious. So long as he could maintain the relationship on that level he was safe. Luther would be getting into position too.

"Where whoa-haw (cattle) you give?"

Forge pointed with his arm, back the way he had come, only swinging it vaguely, indeterminately, eastward. "Long ride," he said. "You come, I give. Cattle, cloth, horses — we make good friends."

"No friends," scoffed the warrior, leaning forward. "No give Comanche. Comanche no come-along you. Make trap — white man have forked tongue black heart. No good."

"I give you. I speak with a good heart. I tell no lie."

As though suddenly finding a word he had been searching for ever since the conversation had begun, the war-leader sat back and said, "Lie! Lie!"

Forge shook his head at the Indian, frowning a trifle. "No lie. I say I give Wasp-Comanche horses, cattle, cloth — I no lie!"

The buck lapsed into a puzzled and thoughtful silence. His eyes went very slowly over Forge's face, over his body and back to his face again, lingered there, then lifted and swept out over the jumbled camp as though seeking outside aid of some kind. After a few moments he looked across at Forge again. "Why you come-along, Foach? No give whoa-haw, no give horses, no give cloth. No give come-along for any. Why?"

"For a little girl," Forge said distinctly, watching for the reaction he expected to see and afraid what the tan face would show. Disappointment perhaps, chagrin — something that would indicate the Comanche couldn't trade.

But the warrior returned Forge's stare with less hostility of a sudden. He rocked back still farther and a crafty glitter showed in his eyes. "You buy-back little girl. You trade many for her. You bring ransom."

The warrior's use of the last word indicated a fully experienced comprehension that indicated he was no novice to the pronunciation or the meaning of it.

"I deliver here — this place. Take time though, take much come-along. Many days, many nights drive many whoa-haws and horses this far. Much work."

The Indian's eyes shone with their rekindled interest. His expression grew shrewd. "How many come-along whoa-haw, horses? How many you come-along cloth? How many you come-along guns?"

"I have no guns," Forge said, making up his mind to give them if he had to, but having a hunch the horses, cattle, and clothing would suffice.

"No gun. Come-along whoa-haw, horses, cloth." The warrior agreed. "How many?"

Forge spread his hands palms downward and shrugged his shoulders. "You have no little white girl — no come-along any."

166

The Comanche smiled for the first time. "Got her," he said. "Got her come-along back. She 'live. She cry get hit — she eat strong."

Forge took a long chance. So far his idea that the raiders would be eager to get usable goods in exchange for Maria was working out, but he still had his doubts. Comanches were cruel, but more than that, they were infinitely treacherous. "You no got her. You lie for horses, whoa-haw, cloth. I don't see her."

But the big buck wasn't angered. His grin lingered, turned more crafty than ever. "She no this camp. She go on. Come-along with hurt braves."

Forge's mind was working fast. The Indians had apparently sent Maria on ahead, if the war-leader wasn't blandly lying. Sent her along with their wounded and injured to the main camp or village. His blue eyes were like daggers when he resumed the bargaining.

"How long take get her back? I no can wait around. Where she go?"

The Comanche was evidently beginning to enjoy the trading. None of his former fierceness showed now. "She come-along one day. I come-along brave get her back. She no far-far now."

He meant the wounded and captives had been very recently sent ahead. This too, coincided with what Forge had heard of Plains Indians. They sent in their wounded and their captives and a majority of their booty before riding on into their main villages themselves. This, in order that, by the time the victorious raiders returned, the mourning was mostly

over with and the distribution of plunder had won back
the people so they would celebrate the victor's return.

If Maria hadn't been gone longer than it would take
one Comanche to ride out and bring her back in one
day's time, it meant she was just exactly far enough out,
to be beyond danger in the fight that was going to come
— unless — she was closer to the main bivouac, in
which case she was in a very bad position. Forge
considered it. He knew questioning the war-leader too
closely would arouse his suspicions, but until he *did*
know where Maria was he would have to be very
careful to do nothing to arouse the Indians or act in any
way that might be interpreted by the Sageland men
hidden and all around them by now, as a signal to start
shooting.

"How far you tepi-town? How come-along you
village?"

The brown eyes seemed to chill and cool a little.
"Why-for?"

"For little girl," Forge said, affecting impatience.
"You no get her back before she get your village. Too
long, too late — no give me time bring back whoa-haw,
horses, cloth."

"Village — no. Village long way. Little girl short way.
We come-along her one day." The Indian made a
motion towards the sun. "No come-along far-far.
Come-along short way."

Forge held out one hand — the left one — palm
upward. Very smartly he reached over with his own
right hand, palm downward, and slapped the left palm.
The noise was an abrupt, sharp sound. "We trade," he

said. "I give Wasp-Comanche one hundred horses. I give Wasp-Comanche three hundred whoa-haws. I give Wasp-Comanche one hundred pants, one hundred red shirts. You give Forge little white girl alive — strong."

"Hau," the Comanche said. "I trade. You bring whoa-haw, horses, cloth, here — this place — one day. I bring little white girl. We make trade."

Forge said, "Take long time. Come-along far off. Take maybe a month drive many whoa-haws, horses, this place. Far-far."

The Comanche raised his shoulders and let them fall in an eloquent gesture. "No come-along fast, I know. Comanches wait. Little white girl grow fat. Plenty good all time. Grow strong. Comanches wait."

Forge sat back and looked steadily at the big buck. He was ready to play his trump card. "I don't know; I haven't seen little girl. You show me her."

This appeared to be logical enough to the Comanche. He held out his own palm and struck it with his other hand, then nodded his head vigorously and got to his feet. "You go," he said. "You go-along warriors. You see little girl. You come-along you village, get whoa-haw, horses, cloth, you come-along back here — this place."

Forge got to his feet with the hope growing strong in his heart. He smiled and struck his palm again, then held his right hand out towards the Comanche. The big Indian struck Forge's right palm with his own left hand. The bargain was sealed.

"You wait."

Forge did. He stood there with weakness running like a fever all through him. She was alive; Maria was alive! In his excitement he looked over where the nearest bucks were. They were studying him as interestedly as he was studying them. The big war-leader was gesturing and grunting out belched words. Forge watched. He wanted the worst way to turn backwards and scrutinise the heat-shimmering distance, westward. If that was the course Maria and the wounded warriors had taken — and if Luther had completed his manoeuvre by now — then Forge was going to lead a band of unsuspecting Comanches to their deaths.

He watched the bucks break up before their leader's harangue. Seven of them headed towards the horse herd. He watched them talk to the horse guards. They caught eight horses but there were only seven Indians, then they led the animals back towards the camp. Puzzled about the eighth animal, Forge understood when he saw the tall war-leader strip the bridle, blanket and saddle off the worn out blaze-faced sorrel and lash the gear to a big sevinna gelding with an ugly head and a mean, treacherous eye. He would have a fresh animal. He exulted inwardly over that, too. It never occurred to him to show fear, although now, when the ordeal was all but over, he was weak-feeling within.

The sevinna was as treacherous in his heart as he was in his appearance. When the war-leader handed Forge the reins, he swung up his left toe and the animal promptly ducked his head and made a vicious swipe at Forge's britches with bared teeth. Anticipating some

170

such unfriendly act, Forge had tightened the off-rein. The horse missed but Forge didn't. Without taking his foot from the stirrup he twisted and lashed out with a fist. It caught the beast on the soft part of his nose. He snorted in pain and threw his head wildly. The Indians howled with laughter. Forge grinned dourly and swung up, took a deep seat and waited, but the horse was convinced; he offered no further signs of rebellion.

The war-leader, still with his little grin, stood beside the sevinna gelding and looked up at Forge. "You come-along braves," he said. "They take you little white girl. You see — you go back — you come-along whoa-haw, horses, cloth. You lie . . ." He stepped back, loosened one hand from the filthy blanket, made a motion of grasping a child by the ankles, swinging it high in the air one-handed, then bringing it down with a terrible impact, crushing out its brains against the ground. To complete the vivid pantomime he reached out with a beaded moccasin and disdainfully kicked the imaginary carcass aside, then looked up at Forge, saying no more.

"I no lie," Forge said slowly, anger burning in him for the cruelty so professionally enacted. "I no lie — you see. Come-along with big surprise for Wasp-Comanches!"

He turned and rode off. The seven warriors were waiting for him. They rode with one rein, most of them, and bareback. They had every kind of weapon and some had even taken time out to daub their chests with Comanche symbols.

Forge led his little cavalcade in a long lope straight towards the westernmost bastion of the valley. Whether he was going in the right direction or not didn't seem to bother the Indians. They followed, apparently content to just lope along in the warmth for a while, before they made known any changes in direction they must follow to overtake the slower moving band of wounded men and their captive white child.

When the camp was small in the distance, Forge turned with a wondering frown and looked at his companions. One of them, a young warrior with a flat, round face, beckoned for him to ride closer to the rest of them. Obediently, Forge swung in beside the Comanche. The buck pointed at the ground and slowly lifted his arm to point out a route directly ahead. Forge saw the tracks as soon as he looked down. They were visible far ahead where the dry, dead grass had been broken and trodden down by horses. He grunted and brought his horse down to a running-walk. The Indians followed his example. Eight men and not a verbal sound from one of them. It was nerve-racking to the white man, whose tension was mounting now that he was on the last lap of a terrible journey.

He kept his eyes fixed on the land ahead. Fear rode with him now, more than it had at the war party's bivouac. If Luther hadn't been watching — if something had happened to prevent the Sageland men from knowing where he was, who he was with, his own position was no better than Maria's. They would both be killed at the first overt sign. It would be ironic if he, the supposed father of the little captive, who had risked so much to get this far, would finally be the cause of her death as well as his own.

He rubbed his eyes with his fists and forced his thoughts to other things. There was bound to be a fight, but it was beginning to look like both he and Maria would be far enough ahead for the noise of shooting to save them from Comanche tomahawks. So, somehow, he had to stay alive and get away from his bodyguards, ride like the wind, find the child, get her, and . . . He saw the movement — only a quick, unguarded flash of sunlight off a weapon. Luther was in place — thank God!

CHAPTER EIGHT

Vengeance is not a Pretty Thing . . .

He lifted the big sevinna horse into a lope and heard the thunder of the Comanche horses behind him. He was as tight in the stomach where the bear meat lay, as a coiled spring. If the Sageland men were along the ridge on his right he could get rid of his companions easily enough, if not . . .

Thinking like that he began to angle his horse closer towards the brush. The young, round-faced buck galloped up beside him and threw him a hard look. Forge made a motion towards the shade over near the foothills, then pointed to the sun above. The Indian appeared to understand although his expression didn't alter. He dropped back a little, where his friends were. They all loped together behind Forge.

It was a bad moment. He knew the Sageland posse's horses were finished. There could be no question of pursuit by the white men. He strained his eyes to find the place where he'd seen the reflection off gun-metal and rode as close to the brushy sidehill as he dared.

174

Few of Luther's men had carbines. Pistol range was very limited. He drew in a deep breath and pushed the sevinna still farther away from the trail they were supposed to be following — then it happened — when he was a good eighty feet from the others, and just when the round-faced warrior's suspicions were fully aroused.

A crashing volley of gunfire that shattered the heatwaves and smashed into the prairie silence like an overdose of thunder.

Forge had a fleeting glimpse of the Sageland men. They jumped up out of the brush and yelled. The pandemonium was complete but Forge's horse kept him fully occupied for several minutes and by the time he was able to turn back, the fight was over.

Of the seven Indians and their mounts, only five bewildered, half-stunned horses were left. He got the ugly brute he was astride under control and was facing eastward, back towards the war party's encampment, when the bucking was done with. Beyond the streaming, triumphant white men, he saw a sight that made his heart turn to lead. A small party of Comanches far back down the trail, were sliding their horses to a dust-spewing halt. For some reason the war-leader had sent others after them. Maybe it was only a hunting party. Whatever it was the damage was done. Even as Forge watched, the Indians overcame their astonishment and let out distantly heard screams of rage, discharged several guns then wheeled their horses and fled back towards the bivouac in a careening race for life.

Forge rode back where the possemen were haggling over the Indian horses and some were lifting Comanche topknots. He swung down when he saw Luther and walked stiff-leggedly towards his brother. The sevinna horse followed him with a sullen and wicked glint in its little eyes.

"Forge! We got 'em!"

"The hell you have," Forge answered back. "There was a little party of them back yonder a ways. They saw the whole thing and lit out for the main camp. You'll have to charge after them and hit the whole camp now before they can get mounted up and organised. Get the men together — hurry up, Lute!"

Luther's mouth hung open. He still had his pistol in his fist and the pallor of excitement under the coating of greasy sweat on his face. "What — ?"

"No time now, Lute." He turned swiftly as a man went by on a chestnut horse. "Here — you; you stay with me." He looked at Luther again. "Dammit, Lute — get up and ride — it's your only chance. Hit 'em before they can get under way. Drive right through 'em. *Hurry up!*"

"But — what'll you do?" Luther asked, toeing into his stirrup and swinging up. "Where'll you be, Forge?"

"Hunting for the wounded. They're up ahead somewhere. If you can, later on, track me. Now go on, Lute. Bust right into them and scatter 'em like quail. Every second counts."

Luther reined away and raised his voice in a thunderous shout at the other men. They retaliated

176

with a triumphant cry of their own and went racing after Luther.

Forge slumped, breathing heavily, holding his lips flat and trying to guess how much of a start the little band of Indians had, then he mounted the sevinna again and swung over towards the abandoned trail of the Comanche wounded.

"You there; come on."

The bareheaded blond man cast a worried look after Luther's band then reluctantly turned and followed after Forge. He wore a tired, anxious expression that had become almost habit by now, to his grey features.

When they were riding side by side Forge said, "What's your name?"

"Paul Showaway. I'm the feller that got them pistol cartridges from you that night back at the Knowlton place."

"Yes," Forge said, "I recollect you all right; just didn't know your name."

"What's up ahead?" Showaway asked. "More Injuns?"

"Yes. They sent their wounded back ahead of the war party. They said the prisoner was up with the wounded."

"The little girl?"

Forge nodded.

"How many d'you reckon there might be, up there?"

Forge looked away from Showaway's face. "I've no idea. If there are too many — why, I reckon we'll just trail 'em and wait for the others to get back. The main

177

thing is — we want to make sure they don't hear what's happened back here and brain their prisoner."

"Yeah," Showaway said absently. "T'wouldn't do, would it?"

Forge didn't answer because he was suddenly confronted with something that angered him deeply, and it was his own oversight that had caused it. Paul Showaway's horse was lagging badly. He looked anxiously from the animal to the man. Showaway's eyes clouded over with an apologetic, worried expression.

"I got to go slow or he'll fold up under me. That last charge out of the brush up there about finished him."

They both reined down to a shambling trot. Forge said, "I'll go ahead. You come after me when you can. If I come across the Indians I'll wait for you — if I can. Keep your eyes peeled. The other ones — the ones back there, will scatter all over the country pretty quick. You don't want to be caught by six or eight of 'em." He jerked his head at the luckless rider and eased off on the sevinna horse. Actually, he wasn't over-worried about Paul Showaway. The Comanches caught between Luther's charge and Waite Hefner's rear-guard would be a while disentangling themselves.

The land lifted gradually towards a V notch that was clearly a pass through the nearing mountains westward. Forge rode up a nearby steep sidehill for a look around, and to his vast surprise and elation the sevinna horse wasn't even breathing hard. As tough as a fried owl, he took miles and mountains with equal aplomb. His ugly head bobbed rhythmically and he hadn't once faltered. Forge left him in the shade of a juniper below the hill's crest and went the last five hundred feet alone. From the eminence he could see the pass through the hills but two closer objects caught and held his attention. One was a southerly, winding, shady-looking willow-lined creek. The other was dark specks far ahead that moved sluggishly towards the pass, but in such a way as to strike the creek first.

He slipped and stumbled back down to the horse, flung up and away again, only now he rode northward on an angling course that would provide him with the dark, splotchy background of the sagebrush hills for protection.

The day wore on. Forge alternated between long gallops and gruelling trots that jarred him unmercifully but gave the rugged Comanche horse a chance to recuperate. Man and animal were perspiring freely and the full wrath of the sun was burning deeply into their salt-stained hides.

The need of the wounded warriors for water finally gave Forge the advantage he needed. He saw the meandering path of the willows across the upper, southern, end of the long valley, and surmised there would be pools along the creek and among the inviting shadows. He watched his prey wind sluggishly in among the willow-shade, and counted them. Eleven astride and four lead-horses which might mean dead Indians tied crossways. That, or plunder.

They rode like they felt, apparently. Slowly, painfully, with an obvious listlessness to them. He left the sevinna horse hidden in a heat-laden swale and flung away from the sweat that ran along his forehead, hearing but

179

unheeding the uneven, slugging cadence of his own heartbeats. He crawled up to the lip of the swale, lay flat and tossed aside his hat. He was as close as he dared get.

Peering cautiously over the little lip of land, eyes squinted against the backlash of sunlight off the yellow-brown cured grass, he studied the Comanches.

Six were laid out flat on the ground. Two were sitting up with improvised splints, one on his right arm the other on his left leg. He guessed the prone warriors were too badly injured to take part in any fighting, and obviously the warrior with the broken right arm wouldn't be much of a threat.

That left four Comanches capable of combat. He lay with the sun baking him, waiting to catch a glimpse of them. The place they had chosen to stop was deep in the shadows. The natural colouring of the warriors and the difficulty of seeing past the willows made his quest impossible. He gave it up with a grunt and settled lower, studying the shadowy places for Maria.

And — he saw her!

Filthy; her dress all but rags and a terrible constricting fear on her face like it was stamped there for ever. Small, unmoving, as silent as any Comanche child would have been, she had apparently learned her Indian lessons well. Clearly she had been struck many times. It showed even at that distance in the cringing, deferential way she stayed out of arm's reach of the wounded men.

While Forge watched, one of the badly injured men made a weak gesture with one hand and Maria leapt up quickly. She knew the sign-talk motion for water. Forge's eyes were squinted almost closed as he watched her scuttle, child-like, to the cool water, snatch up a carelessly dropped gourd, fill it and hurry back to the wounded man.

But she was hesitant about approaching. Forge could understand — almost feel — her terror of approaching too close to the dying Indian. She held out the gourd to him. He reached for it but was too weak. Another warrior, his shoulders caked with stiff blood from the side of his head where a leaf-poultice was secured over a huge swelling, growled at her and swung his hand viciously. She ducked back quickly, then went still closer to the prone man. Forge swore once, drew out his hand-gun, laid it level with the ground and tugged back the hammer with fury showing around his mouth.

The Indian with the bandaged head raised his voice louder. It happened in a flash. He swung his arm like a streak. She was pitifully small and un-agile. The blow was audible where Forge lay. Maria's wavering little bleat hung in the stifling air just for a moment. Forge's shot blasted the heatwaves with a stunning explosion. The Comanche with the bandaged head spun crazily and threw his hands straight out in front of him as though to ward off a blow. He tried to take a small step, then he fell like a log and didn't move again.

Forge's caution told him — when he was aiming the gun — that what he was doing was madness, but he pulled off the shot just the same. After the Indian fell, he watched with eyes like a hawk's the dismay he had caused among the other bucks.

Maria, like the badly wounded Comanches, lay on the ground too petrified to move. Forge gripped his gun tighter, waiting, never letting his glimpse of her waver. The Indians who were able had struggled to their feet and one, with a roar, leapt at the small girl with a knife shining dully in the shade.

That was Forge's second shot.

The warrior was knocked sideways, hit in the neck. He sprawled near the creek, threshing frantically.

Forge dragged back the hammer for the third time and waited with the gunbutt slippery in his grip and the sweat stinging his eyes, concentrating on Maria. But the other Indians had had enough. He knew it when he heard the wild scramble of racing horses. Then he dared to fling off the sweat and relax his grip on the pistol a little.

He didn't move for a long time. Not until he was satisfied the other Comanches, the badly wounded ones, weren't waiting for him. He edged up over the lip of the swale using the sevinna horse as a shield. Worked his way right up to the deathly silent place where stony black eyes watched helplessly as he approached. No one fired at him.

He was shaking badly by the time he dared to tie the horse and ease himself into full view of the remaining warriors. Even his hands trembled. He cocked the pistol with his thumb and stepped boldly up in front of the Comanches.

A dying Indian fixed him with eyes that shone with hatred and began a reedy, nasal, death chant. It made Forge's flesh creep. He made a gesture towards the

Indian indicating he wasn't going to harm him. The warrior never wavered in either his hating glare nor his chant. It was almost as though he were taunting Forge to kill him.

"Maria?"

He watched her sit up. In that setting she was pitifully small, abysmally afraid and big-eyed. He got his first shock when she looked up at him with the bluest eyes he had ever seen. A shade of blue made softer, deeper, more compelling, by the shadows they were in. He winced a little, unconsciously. Once he had known eyes like those; just once. His mother's eyes. That his own were the identical shape and colour escaped him at that moment.

"Maria? Come over here by me."

She stared without moving and a long trembling shiver passed through her. Forge shook his head at her, gently.

"They won't hurt you. They're gone — all but these." He waved the pistol towards the six badly wounded men lying side by side. Another one was chanting his death song too, but the voice was huskily weak, like a tired wind in the treetops. He was fast dying and knew it. The white man — the little white girl — didn't matter. Nothing mattered; just the ritual of announcing to the Spirit World that a Comanche warrior was coming very soon.

Forge wanted to make the Indians stop their keening but he didn't know how to tell them to. He raised his glance and studied the shimmering distances westward and eastward. There wasn't a movement or a sign of life anywhere. He looked back at the little girl.

"Come on, Maria. Get up and walk over here by me. The Indians won't hurt you."

She got up finally, which was more than he expected after seeing the shock in her face, stood very straight and sturdy and gazed at him owlishly. There was a long, uneven welt from her hairline half way down her cheek. Forge glanced briefly at the man who had caused it and found the thought of his death a pleasant thing.

Maria moved towards him but stopped just out of arm's reach. She was poised for flight, big-eyed and showing a wistful hope — faith, almost — that this would be a different kind of a man. Forge knelt and smiled at her. With the prickling of his beard he saw himself in his mind's eye and understood her timidity. He might be a white man and a rescuer, but he was also a frighteningly villainous-looking spectacle to a very little girl with terror in the forefront of her mind.

He said, "I tell you what, Maria. If you'll get *me* a couple of gourds of that water, I'll wash my face and maybe I won't look so terrible." He was smiling. It was startling how much his face and his brother's face had in common when he smiled, only there was no one but a little girl to see it now, and she wouldn't know.

"I'll give you this, if you'll get me the water." He held out a shiny coin and it didn't seem to Forge, right then, that money had ever had such a formidable value before. He waited, and very timorously, Maria smiled at him.

184

And there was further proof. He recognised it instantly. The warm, gentle smile of the Windsors. It was shining out of the bruised soreness of her face. Past the tear stains and the dirt, the smudges and the thick coating of dun-dust. The Windsor smile. No wonder CarrieLee had said her daughter reminded her of things long past. He was looking into his own face, almost.

He watched her go to the creek, fill the gourds and bring them back to him one at a time. She had to purse her lips and scowl just the smallest bit, and use both hands to support a filled gourd, but she did it with all the sombre gravity of an older person. He handed her the coin, watched her put it in the middle of her palm and regard it with considerable solemnity, then he bent to wash. He felt cleaner if he didn't especially look it, but by then it didn't matter. She was won over.

He stood up stiffly, loosened the cincha of the Comanche horse and went over where the wounded bucks were. One, he saw, was dead. He guessed it was the one who had been chanting in the weak voice. Another one was very close to death's door and of the four remaining alive he was the sickest looking.

Maria tagged along at his heels, her eyes glistening with the same warm, adoring glow that a puppy's eyes show for a master who can do no wrong.

One Indian stared at him with unwavering and very clear hostility. He lingered longest by that warrior. It was as though the warm insect-laden air among the willows was filled with the Comanche's quenchless flame of hatred. Forge bent quickly, grasped the buck's blanket, jerked it roughly aside and looked at the ashen, wasted body beneath. The Indian had been shot through the soft-parts. There was a milky fluid lying in the hollows of his abdomen near a full length tear in his lower intestines area.

Forge lowered the blanket and looked into the man's face. It appeared for just the fleetingest of seconds, as though a dreaded question lay deep in the black eyes. As though to answer, Forge raised and lowered his shoulders and shook his head slowly. The Indian understood. His grey lips moved to form a word and the blanket twitched futilely on each side of his body where his arms lay. Forge bent down, took Maria's hand and moved away.

A sense of overwhelming fatigue permeated him. He walked up the creek with the little girl and, true to the effervescence that is strongest in the very young, Maria found her tongue and spirits at the same time. She tugged at him, eager to explore the glades they passed through, and talked in a torrent of words. He listened without answering, feeling the old pain coming back stronger than ever.

They were eating buffalo jerky from the litter of packs left behind by the warriors who had fled, when Forge saw the riders coming through the filagree of willow branches. They were fanned out in a long, in-curving circle, coming straight for the creek. He was sure they were the Sageland men but with caution he drew Maria far back into the shady places and knelt near her, waiting.

It was Luther. The Texan was riding with him. A little behind them was Paul Showaway on an Indian horse, his unkempt blond hair as unruly and tangled as ever.

Forge turned with a little smile and was shocked by the imprint of terror on Maria's face. He reached out and put a heavy hand on her shoulder. "It's friends, honey. Now we'll go home."

Her eyes flashed with quick intentness. "Back to mother and daddy and Willie and Junior?"

The recollection of Asa Knowlton lying in the wavering red-gold firelight snagged at his mind. "Back to mother," he said, and stood up looking at the horsemen. Luther was in the lead. "Come on; we'll walk out so they'll know where we are." They did and Luther's face curled into a slow smile. He dismounted amid the flying dust and dropped to one knee.

"Are you Maria?"

She responded instantly to the gentleness he radiated. "Yes. Who are you? Are you a friend of — his?" She looked up at Forge.

"I sure am, honey. I'm his brother."

"I have a brother," she said quickly. "Two brothers and a mother and a —"

Forge said, "Now we can all go back." He was looking down at Luther who got unsteadily to his feet and dusted automatically at his knee. "What happened back there, Lute?"

"Like shooting sitting ducks," Luther said. "Waite turned the trick. They were trying to get mounted up to charge us when he bowled them over. They scattered all right like you said they would, but there are a lot of them that didn't. They're still back there." He looked down at Maria and was silent for a moment, then looked up at Forge and went on again.

"Good thing for us they did scatter, too. We were outnumbered about two to one. There were closer to eighty than sixty of them. Must have been a hundred in their war party when they struck out." Luther looked towards the willows where some Comanche horses stood drowsily, lean-flanked and primitive-looking where the war paint had merged with their sweat. "What happened in there?"

"Shot a couple. Another one or two rode off and there are four or five others that're dying."

Luther dropped his horse's reins and went forward. Forge didn't go back with him. He and Maria went into the shade and watched the Sageland men come trooping in out of the sunshine. Waite Hefner winked very solemnly at Maria then grinned crookedly at Forge.

"Well — we done it after all, but by God I don't mind telling you I had my doubts plenty of times."

"We all did," Forge said. "Did you boys lose any men back there?"

Hefner shook his head. "Three horses is all. Oh — Mort Stevens sprained his ankle when his horse went down, but outside of that we're all fit as a fiddle and danged eager to get back where that Comanche jerky's piled and waitin'."

"Did you stop to change horses?" Forge could see that most of the men had Indian mounts.

188

"Yeah. We bunched up the other stock too. 'Pick 'em up on the way back, Lute says."

Forge nodded. "You didn't happen to see anything of that war-leader did you? Big feller, looked like he was a cross-bred of some kind; lighter than the rest of them. He spoke Comanche-English."

"Well — if it's the big buck that had his hair done up in rat hides or weasel skins, or whatever in hell they were, yeah — I saw him. I saw him right over my front sight and blew his dog-eating heart out."

Forge turned when Luther came back and touched his arm with a worried expression. "What'll we do with those?" Luther asked. "Can't just leave them there — can we?"

Forge frowned. He had no answer to that. It was Waite Hefner who broke the silence. "Yeah; if we stick around and try to patch 'em up they'll just die anyway. If we ride off and leave 'em their people will come back and get them. Comanches never leave their dead unburied or the wounded unattended. There's no worry there." The Texan was regarding Luther's expression of concern as though it mildly disgusted him. After all — those *were* damned Comanche Indians . . .

Forge said, "I think he's right, Lute."

"Well; we can head back then."

They did, but first they stopped at the abandoned Comanche camp and filled up on jerky, took what caught their eyes, then rounded up the big horse-herd and struck out. The way back, though, was longer than Forge had thought it would be. Longer than he had anticipated because of two things. One, the Indian horses were no end of trouble as soon as they hit the sage country again. Like all western horses they ducked their heads low and tried to slip away in the brush where the riding was the toughest for the men who were profanely trying to herd them.

The second delay was occasioned by settlers they encountered near the burnt out ranch, not far from Asa Knowlton's grave. One, a bearded patriarch with a fiery eye, listened to Forge's recital of what they had found when they swept by the night of the attack, and what they had done to the marauders when they finally caught up to them. It mollified the old man a little. The dead people were his son and daughter-in-law and two small children, one still in the cradle.

The old man was a preacher-of-sorts. He insisted on saying a long, dolorous prayer over Asa Knowlton's grave. Forge tried to dissuade him but he persisted so the Sageland men stood around bareheaded, grimy, worn out and saddle-weary, with their heads bowed and their eyes fixed on the face of a little girl who looked on in rapt silence — until the old settler said, ". . . the earthly remains of Asa Knowlton."

Forge longed to kneel and hold her hand and when he saw the whiteness of understanding steal into her face, he did. He took her in close and surrounded her with man-strength.

She understood that the man she called father was under the freshly made mound with its dark, moist-looking richness, but she didn't cry and that amazed them all.

190

She was soberly silent when they took up their homeward trail again, later, and Forge felt she was holding it back. He got that impression from the way her eyes would turn from one man's grimy face to another. Each man was kindness itself in their different ways, but they were strangers.

Luther rode with Forge and Maria once in a while. He could almost always get a little, wan smile from the child, where she perched like a knot on a log astraddle the gaudy Comanche-decorated Mexican saddle Forge had given her out of the Indian plunder. He was riding with them when they finally came up over the swell of the last hill and could see the great plains rolling onward to the horizon — wind-whipped now and with hurrying grey clouds scudding by overhead, ragged and swollen-looking with the coming of winter. North of the immense flow of flat country, tucked up in its own rolling corner of the Universe, was Sageland, like a huge beehive that reflected the sun off its newness.

"Home," Luther said. The way he said it conveyed a lot of meaning. Maria felt it. Forge winced when she swung eagerly and looked down where the Knowlton ranch was — had been. There was nothing left but scorched places like black wounds. He saw the way she stared and urged his horse up a little.

"Pretty soon now you'll see your mother and your brothers and I've got something for you, too. I've got a little sorrel horse with a flaxen mane and tail. He's a little feller — weigh maybe six-fifty, seven hundred pounds. We'll get a saddle somewhere. There's a saddlemaker in town. Maybe we could get him to make you a saddle. One with nickel spots and conchos on it."

"And — white strings?"

"And white strings, by golly." He shot a glance at Luther and beyond. The Knowlton place was sliding away rearwards. His brother was looking straight ahead with his eyes puckered up.

"Yes, and white strings, too, and a bridle to match. Why — Maria — I reckon you'll be the prettiest girl in Sageland — don't you?"

She said, "Will my mother like it? She said when she was a little girl she always wanted a horse of her own and a saddle like that — with white strings and shiny conchos."

"I reckon she'll like it, honey," Forge said. "I reckon she will."

They came down the slope and hit the clearings. They drove their Comanches horses and personal, worn-out mounts as far as Waite Hefner's place and corralled them there and left Waite, too. The Texan smiled and waved to his wife who was standing motionlessly watching him, then he went over slowly to Forge and held out his hand.

"Forge — I tell you honestly I've seen you a lot in town. I never cared much for what I seen either. Well — I'm here to say a man's a fool when he judges another man by appearances and hearsay. Shake."

Forge shook. He wasn't exactly surprised but he was very embarrassed. It wasn't until they were riding down the wagon ruts again that led into town that he recalled Waite Hefner's early coolness and speculative glances, and now the wonder of why Hefner had had such feelings bothered him.

He waited until he and Maria were up with Luther, then he mentioned it.

"Lute? I'm not very popular around the country, am I?"

"Oh," Lute said in his warm, slow way, "I wouldn't say that, Forge. You've never given folks much of a chance to know you, is about all."

Forge studied Luther's face for a second then smiled crookedly. "You're not a very good liar, Lute," he said.

Luther matched his grin. "What'd you expect me to say? — We're kin you know."

"You aren't proud of it though."

"That's not true," Luther said. "Not true at all. There've been plenty of times when I thought you needed a darned good hiding, but like I've always figured with men like you, Forge, — life'll knock you down enough times without me having to do it."

"How do you mean, Lute?"

Luther let his gaze drop a little to Maria. She was riding as erect as an adult but her legs didn't reach much below the saddleskirts. He kept his eyes on her face for a moment then raised them to Forge again. "Like that," he said, and squeezed his horse's sides, riding ahead a little so he wouldn't have to go any further into the conversation.

Forge was looking after his brother's retreating back when his attention was drawn away by shouts far ahead. Almost before the sight of the hard riding townsmen coming out to meet them had died, the fire bell in Sageland went into wild paroxyms of frenzied clanging. It sounded wonderful to all the returning men but Forge. He saw the distant advance of the possemen mingle with those who had raced out from town to welcome them home. The prospect of such back-thumping appalled him. He looked down at Maria and saw her eyes widen. He leaned a little from the waist and reined over closer to her.

"Honey — let's you and me streak it around the edge of all this and head for town by the north road. What say?"

"Yes," she said lingeringly, absorbed in the confusion and bedlam far ahead.

"Let's go then," Forge said, lifting the ugly sevinna horse into his rocketing lope and watching her drum sturdily with naked heels on her own mount.

They rode all the way around the crowds that were swarming out to greet the returning heroes, galloping in the opposite direction. When Forge looked back once he saw the swarming people surrounding Luther with howls and blows of commendation, then Luther was lost in the bedlam.

They made it to the north road without anything more serious obstructing their progress than a few frenzied waves beckoning them to come back and Forge watched Maria ride with her blue eyes squinted against the gusty atmosphere she was journeying through. The Windsor look . . .

"MISTER WINDSOR!" The liveryman was beside himself. His three gold teeth fairly sparkled with geniality. A younger man came up, eyed Forge's horse and looked up at the rider.

"Dang. Not much of a trade."

Forge remembered. He said, "Your blaze-faced sorrel's as tough a little horse as there is in the country, pardner. He's out at Hefner's where we left the loosestock. I'll have him brought into town after a bit." He paused, thrust a hand into his pocket and withdrew some limp, bedraggled bills, peeled off two fifties and handed them to the wide-eyed man. "That's for the use of him. He's pretty well tucked up but that'll help feed him back up again."

"Lord, Mister Windsor," the younger man said, "I only paid seventeen dollars for him over in Fontaine two years back."

Forge swung off the big Comanche horse, regarded it dourly then wagged his head. "Turn him out, will you? He's the ugliest animal I ever rode and meaner'n a snake — but tough. I'll just sort of keep him around to look at." He helped Maria down. She rubbed her legs gingerly and looked up at him with a pained smile she couldn't hide.

"I'm glad we're home," she said simply. "I need chaps if I ever have to do *that* again."

Forge grinned and the fat liveryman doubled over and the younger man holding the two fifty dollar bills laughed. "I hope you never have to, honey," the liveryman said in a deep, booming voice, "but if you do — why — you be sure to have that man right there to ride along with you."

195

Forge felt embarrassed. There was a warmth in the men's eyes he had trouble facing. He was grateful for the admiration and acceptance but his neck was red when he reached down hastily and took Maria's hand. "Come on, Maria; we've got to see that saddlemaker."

He led her out into the shade on the west side of the road, which was all but deserted, and heard the distant racket of the impromptu celebration at the far end of town. He kept his head down and led Maria along as fast as he dared, towards the saddle shop. The saddlemaker himself was standing in the doorway, watching southward, when Forge spoke to him. "Will — here's a young lady that's just got to have a pair of chaps made to order and right now. And after that she's got to have — ."

"Mister Windsor!" The man's astonishment was complete with popping eyes. "I — you ought to be down there with your brother. Is this Maria? Why — folks been talkin' about you two a solid two weeks now. That and nothin' else. Come on in, Maria — chaps? Why bust my buttons if we don't make you the fanciest g — oldanged chaps in the whole territory."

"And Will," Forge said, "we want a black saddle with nickel spots and shiny conchos and — ."

"White strings," Maria said swiftly, her eyes aglow. "And a bridle to match — with white strings!"

The saddlemaker sat down slowly and gazed from Maria to Forge. Forge could see what was coming; it was in the man's eyes. He sought swiftly for a way out. "Will — I'll leave her here for a second with you — you

196

can sort of take down what she wants. I'll — I'll be right back."

He rushed out into the roadway, saw the alarming spectacle of Sageland staging a wild celebration, got the feeling it wasn't altogether spontaneous, and made a quick dash for his office. Inside it was quiet. The clerks weren't even there. Quiet and cool.

"Forge."

He turned. She was standing back from the window looking at him. Motionless, almost without expression, her hands interlocked and held so tightly that the knuckles showed white — alone.

"CarrieLee."

"I was watching from upstairs. I saw you ride around them and go to the liverybarn with Maria. I watched both of you walk over to the saddlemaker's shop." She gripped her fingers tighter. There were purple shadows under her eyes. "I know about Asa."

"You know?" he said dumbly. "How?"

"Luther sent a man in ahead of the rest of you yesterday. He's — very thoughtful."

"Oh." He understood then, why the townsmen were expecting them when they came draggingly over the far-off ridge. He nodded. "Lute — well — he always was good at thinking ahead."

"Forge — you don't want my thanks, I know, and I couldn't thank you anyway. There aren't any words; if there are I don't know them. There's nothing I can say, Forge — that you'd understand. But it'll always live in me. Thank you for bringing her back alive."

She didn't move and neither did he. All the haunting moments he'd had were making it difficult for him to think and making it even more impossible for him to speak. He tried, though.

"CarrieLee . . ." He choked over the name, floundered and finally fell silent looking at her.

She went closer to read his face and got a strange, rapt expression. "Did you see it, Forge?"

"I saw it, CarrieLee. You said you and God wouldn't let me forget. I didn't know how you meant that. I'm sorry, CarrieLee — I know now — I'm sorry."

She dropped her gaze. He thought she was going to turn away and said, "No; wait, CarrieLee. I want to ask you to forgive me for everything I've done. To marry me."

She lifted her glance again. "Asa's boys, Forge. They're my responsibility now, too."

"I know. I thought it all out on the way back home. Asa's boys, too, CarrieLee. I owe him that and more. Will you marry me, CarrieLee?"

"Oh — Yes! Forge — yes!"

He held her like he had once before, years back. Was still holding her, neither of them saying a word, when Luther came to the door, stopped stock-still, then turned away and motioned the crowd away too.

They both heard and even saw a little of it and didn't care. Not for a long time, and neither of them spoke at all until Forge turned a little to hide his face in the afternoon shadows and said, "Let's go get Maria and our boys."

198

About the Author

Lauran Paine who, under his own name and various pseudonyms, has written over 900 books, was born in Duluth, Minnesota, a descendant of the Revolutionary War patriot and author, Thomas Paine. His family moved to California when he was at an early age and his apprenticeship as a Western writer came about through the years he spent in the livestock trade, rodeos, and even motion pictures where he served as an extra because of his expert horsemanship in several films starring movie cowboy Johnny Mack Brown. In the late 1930s, Paine trapped wild horses in northern Arizona and even, for a time, worked as a professional farrier. Paine came to know the Old West through the eyes of many who had been born in the previous century and he learned that Western life had been very different from the way it was portrayed on the screen. "I knew men who had killed other men," he later recalled. "But they were the exceptions. Prior to and during the Depression, people were just too busy eking out an existence to indulge in Saturday-night brawls." He served in the U.S. Navy in the Second World War and began writing for Western pulp magazines following his discharge. It is interesting to note that all of his earliest novels (written under his own name and the pseudonym Mark Carrel) were published in the British market and he soon had as strong a following in that country as in the United States. Paine's Western fiction is characterized by strong plots, authenticity, an apparently effortless ability to construct situation and character, and a preference for building his stories upon a solid foundation of historical fact. ADOBE EMPIRE (1956), one of his best novels, is a fictionalized account of the last twenty years in the life of trader William Bent and, in an off-trail way, has a melancholy, bittersweet texture that is not easily forgotten. MOON PRAIRIE (1950), first published in the United States in 1994, is a memorable story set during the mountain man period of the frontier. In later novels such as THE HOMESTEADERS (1986) or THE OPEN RANGE MEN (1990), he showed that the special magic and power of his stories and characters had only matured along with his basic themes of changing times, changing attitudes, learning from experience, respecting nature, and the yearning for a simpler, more moderate way of life. His most recent Western novels have been published as Five Star Westerns and include LOCKWOOD, THE WHITE BIRD, CACHE CAÑON, and THE MUSTANGERS.

ISIS publish a wide range of books in large print, from fiction to biography. Any suggestions for books you would like to see in large print or audio are always welcome. Please send to the Editorial Department at:

ISIS Publishing Limited
7 Centremead
Osney Mead
Oxford OX2 0ES

A full list of titles is available free of charge from:

Ulverscroft Large Print Books Limited

(UK)
The Green
Bradgate Road, Anstey
Leicester LE7 7FU
Tel: (0116) 236 4325

(Australia)
P.O. Box 314
St Leonards
NSW 1590
Tel: (02) 9436 2622

(USA)
P.O. Box 1230
West Seneca
N.Y. 14224-1230
Tel: (716) 674 4270

(Canada)
P.O. Box 80038
Burlington
Ontario L7L 6B1
Tel: (905) 637 8734

(New Zealand)
P.O. Box 456
Feilding
Tel: (06) 323 6828

Details of **ISIS** complete and unabridged audio books are also available from these offices. Alternatively, contact your local library for details of their collection of **ISIS** large print and unabridged audio books.